CW01667751

MY BAGS ARE BIG

ALSO BY TIBOR FISCHER

NOVELS

Under the Frog (1992)

The Thought Gang (1994)

The Collector Collector (1997)

Voyage to the End of the Room (2003)

Good to be God (2008)

The Hungarian Tiger (2014)

How to Rule the World (2018)

SHORT STORIES

Don't Read This Book If You're Stupid (2000)

Crushed Mexican Spiders (2011)

TIBOR FISCHER

MY BAGS ARE BIG

SALT

CROMER

PUBLISHED BY SALT PUBLISHING 2026

2 4 6 8 10 9 7 5 3 1

Copyright © Tibor Fischer 2026

Tibor Fischer has asserted his right under the Copyright, Designs and Patents Act 1988 to be identified as the author of this work.

This book is sold subject to the condition that it shall not, by way of trade or otherwise, be lent, resold, hired out, or otherwise circulated without the publisher's prior consent in any form of binding or cover other than that in which it is published and without a similar condition including this condition being imposed on the subsequent publisher.

This book is a work of fiction. Any references to historical events, real people or real places are used fictitiously. Other names, characters, places and events are products of the author's imagination, and any resemblance to actual events or places or persons, living or dead, is entirely coincidental.

First published in Great Britain in 2026 by
Salt Publishing Ltd
12 Norwich Road, Cromer, Norfolk NR27 0AX, United Kingdom

GPSR representative
Matt Parsons matt.parsons@upi2mbooks.hr
UPI-2M PLUS d.o.o., Medulićeva 20, 10000 Zagreb, Croatia

www.saltpublishing.com

Salt Publishing Limited Reg. No. 5293401

A CIP catalogue record for this book is available from the British Library

ISBN 978 1 78463 385 1 (Paperback edition)
ISBN 978 1 78463 386 8 (Electronic edition)

Typeset in Neacademia by Salt Publishing

Printed and bound in Great Britain by Clays Ltd, Elcograf S.p.A.

FSC
www.fsc.org
MIX
Paper | Supporting responsible forestry
FSC® C018072

For My Big Cousin

O *quantum est in rebus inane!*
(How much emptiness there is in things.)
—LUCILIUS

Come and have a go if you think you're hard enough.
—Unknown English Football Hooligan

BITCOIN WAS SIX cents or so at the time. But I didn't know that. Almost no one did.

I saw him first. For a moment I wasn't sure. But it was Jasper. Worn, but still with hair on top. Only lightly slapped by time. And the bounce. Jasper was walking on the other side of Old Compton Street. Carrying a briefcase. He'd probably been at some meeting, flashing some proposal. Is Soho still the lair of the film business? I don't know. As usual, Jasper was in good spirits.

That's the benefit of being cheery, seeing chance as your chum. And being good at meetings. Jasper . . . he was an enricher of meetings, passing round the hope. You might not be as successful as you'd like, but if you can mix manfully, you'll probably be in the running.

I used to be quite good at it too. Find someone's opinion on something, skiing, cauliflower, watches, whatever, and agree with it. For Jasper it was natural. For me it was tactics. Nearly always entry-level, we're-all-mates, we're-cut-from-the-same-cloth stuff like that. But I could up the bonding on occasion. You're a Gemini? What? So am I! Thought so. You grew up in Southampton? That's funny, so did I. That sort of porky needs careful note-taking and management, however.

Then there is the other school of thought. Maybe the best way to influence is the opposite. If you're friendly, you're probably weak and want something. If you've just bloodied my nose, you're strong and worth getting to know. Someone said so, somewhere, sometime.

Rough em up. But that's high risk and tricky to apply.

The same with beautiful women. Ignoring. Laying on the ignoring with a goddess is a great tactic, but it's tricky to apply.

Moving to another city is serious ignoring, but if she doesn't know you, she may not be swayed.

Parrish deployed major coolness once; he arranged, at great effort and expense, to be trapped in a lift with the office looker. Parrish sat there for three hours with her, not saying a word, gazing at the lift specifications. It didn't get him anywhere. Nothing guarantees anything.

Jasper's films haven't been in cinemas that have audiences, or got anywhere, I know that. Late at night, when I can't sleep, I've gone to the computer and looked him up. I couldn't be arsed to track them down, but Jasper's had a couple of releases. That's over, what, twenty plus years? But you can't complain if you get a release.

For a moment, I thought I'd walk on, before he logged me. But why?

"Jasper," I shout, and since I'd been badly done over by time: "It's me, Dan."

"Dan. Hello. I've been out rustling up some finance for a bio about Julius Caesar, war crime artist," Jasper explained.

"Swords and sandals galore then. Shields too."

"Not really. It a two-hander, set in a cottage outside Pompei."

We slung some slang. We had a joint guffaw about the centre-halves at Manchester United. We cursed the England team for being dozy and overpaid.

We shook the dust off some acquaintances. Divorces. Surprising shagging. Cancers. Disappearances into Wales. We grumbled about prices in London. We agreed the Mayor was a twat. An enormous twat. A true volunteer twat. Jasper recommended a new Tibetan restaurant; I traded him a place that did a great goat curry.

I was wondering whether Jasper would mention Vikki or ask me about her. Jasper didn't. Their divorce had been so fierce (fury over the division of the garden hose etc.), the lawyers stripping both naked, and pulling out their fillings, not surprising he didn't want to go there.

Late at night, when I can't sleep, I've gone to the computer and looked her up. Found nothing. Except for possibly a harsh review on Amazon for a food mixer written by a Vikki without a surname.

"We must do lunch, we must," he said as a farewell.

Chatting with Jasper was weirdly bracing. It cheered me. Yeah, Jasper's good at meetings. That's in his bag of tools.

Jasper bounced off, completely unaware that what, twenty plus years ago? I had made very detailed plans to kill him.

WE WERE HAVING a dismal drink one evening, not long after my mother had died when my father told me that they had tossed a coin. Whether or not to have a second child. "Your brother was such a nightmare." After a moment, he continued: "Perhaps I shouldn't have told you that."

But what is family for, if not entertainment? I only really go back to London now to embarrass my son. It's hilarious. So many ways to wind him up.

฿

Bitcoin is around twenty thousand dollars or so. Almost everyone knows that. They say it's a bear market. They have to say something.

Dorset crab or Wienerschnitzel? Okay, when you're in Dubai, you should give the camel burger a go, but frankly the Dorset crab and Wienerschnitzel are now as Dubai as the Bedouin stuff.

"Tell me about crypto," says Vikki. "Mandy says both you and Ming are crypto fiends. She calls you the prophet of profit."

I'm asked a lot about crypto. When I'm asked to talk about crypto, I'm usually not being asked to talk about life under the Merkle trees, what I'm usually being asked is: direct me directly to the riches. Tell me quickly, how to coin it quickly. Tales of ker-ching. How do I get big, superinflating bags and face-melting gains so I can get a private army and tell everyone what I think of them? Safely? How can I unbitch myself? Can I beat the Wheel? The immediate?

Some people are trawling for crypto disasters, a bit of

misery-tourism. So-and-so lost his job, his home, his wife and kids, his friends, every penny? Wow. Witnessing how others are much more stupid and unfortunate than you is always a blast, a pick-me-up.

Vikki isn't interested in that. It's more what have you been up to? In the way an adult might ask small kids what they've been doing all day.

"Crypto . . ." I say.

I hesitate where to start, I also hesitate between the Dorset crab and the Wienerschnitzel. As I hesitate there's war 'n' starvation in besieged Ukrainian towns. Non-stop executions of women and kids. The abduction of fridges. Extremely unnecessary activities that the Russians have revived. Horrors from the history books. Dark-age doings. Was it all avoidable? Oh, yeah. Do I have any discomfort about my menu predicament? No.

You want to make sure that you're in the right place, at the right time. Hesitating between the Dorset crab and the Wienerschnitzel, in a cool restaurant in Dubai, that's right place, a right time, not sizzling the dog cutlet in a Mariupol cellar.

"Dubai is number one," says the young Brit at the next table.

What I dislike about this place is that you're packed in like tinned sardines and that you're splashed with the flanking jabber. Dubai number one? Could be. But for how long? This week? This month? This year? Dubai number one? Someone simply having the confidence to say that loudly in public, says a lot. But number one at what?

The number one place in the world where diners sit in restaurants telling each other that they're number one? Dubai is certainly in the running for the number one place to show off your trinkets. Or to show off your arse, if you have a showable arse. And even if you don't. Always worth a try. Everyone gets a fan club. Beat the Wheel if you can.

The centre-of-the-universe show. It's getting a rousing revival in Dubai. Crypto is life times ten, and when your bags are big, and you've been around, you know being number one doesn't mean much. You've learned that there's nothing holding up the scenery, so, take some profits. Take some profits. Have the crab, have the Wienerschnitzel. Have both. Twice. If you are number one, don't forget, there's only one direction left to go in.

I'm tempted by the crab, but it's usually not a proper serving. Mostly salad with specks of crab. It's one of those starters that's pushed its way onto the mains. For eaters who don't truly want to eat. Something to play with while they hobnob and jangle their trinkets. Although your typical weight-watcher now would want an extra dollop of virtue to go with that.

If you're not pigging out, you have to choose something veggie or even better vegan. Vegan's harder. A bold warrior gesture. From a small table in Dubai, you're giving evil a kicking. Giving the lords of darkness one in the cobblers. You're not lunching, you're in hand-to-hand combat with the forces of evil. Correcting everything. Via a few chickpeas on your fork. Or carrots.

The Wienerschnitzel will never let you down. You're not walking away wanting more or feeling cheated. But occasionally, I do fancy crab.

At the next table, the young Brit is now talking to a much older Brit about crypto. We're so close, much as I want to, I can't block him out.

"Most crypto is rubbish, of course," he's saying. "But there are blue-chip cryptos, like Bitcoin and Ethereum, they're the smart play."

What he's saying is true, but it's entry-level. By the sound of it, he's spent ten hours watching stuff, read a few articles, maybe even one book (but only an ultra-slim one for the dozy, with plenty of pictures).

It's not academic. The young guy's selling something. He's got that dogged tempo, the dogged tempo of the salesman. To the man who knows nothing about crypto, the man who has watched ten hours of videos on crypto is wise.

Blockchain. Smart Contracts. Staking. Friedrich Hayek. Metaverse. Layer One. Layer two. All that. His patter is touring all the highlights of crypto. The older Brit is nodding off. He'll probably invest to shut the young guy up.

Yes or no? Should I intervene? Should I lean over and say you don't need someone to invest for you. Because the whole point of crypto is the do-it-yourself. All you need is a phone or a laptop. But we do like middlemen, we like others to do the work. To pour the tea. To hold our hand. We like someone we can scream at if things go pear-shaped.

If I leaned over and flashed some knowledge, whose life would change the most? The young guy or the codger? For the better or worse? Doors often have helpful signs, readable, clear guidance. Pull. Push. How to proceed. Life could use some signposting.

Push? Pull? Hard to say. As we all discover, sometimes what hits like bad luck isn't. Or is, but diverts you to some tasty good luck. And vice-versa. Maybe malleting the sales pitch will transfer the crypto shiller to a better occupation, opening an orphanage or sheltering stray cats somewhere. Maybe my flash will send Mr Crumbly into poverty because he missed the boat on crypto, the rocket to the moo-oon.

So many of us are here in Dubai. Crypto vets. The survivors. The lifers. Dubai is a cross between Las Vegas, an airport departure lounge and a pirate bay. Sunshine and no tax. What can you get away with here? Hard to say, but a lot. A lot more than in many other cities. They love gold. Pearls. Trade. Wads. Ostentation cherished here. Asylum for the loaded. Advantage is pretty. In Dubai, advantage is pretty, as some immigration guy remarked to me.

"Crypto? Very volatile," I say to Vikki. "I'd stay away from crypto if I were you." I'll start with the stonewall. See how she plays that.

"I went to the Burj this morning. Had to," chuckles Vikki. "It's simply the world's biggest cock, isn't it?"

They have the world's biggest cock here. They erected the tallest skyscraper, the Burj Khalifa. Look, our cock is the biggest. We have the biggest one, beholders. It's a very simple, multi-language boast. The Saudis are, were? planning a bigger one, but maybe even they recognized that waving your willy at the sky, doesn't get you anywhere. Indeed, it may be advertising for trouble.

"As cocks go, it's a bit thin. You want some heft," Vikki says. "It looks a bit wobbly."

"Rather like Dubai then,' I reply.

"You do get to see everything from the top. Slightly disappointing. I suppose you have to do it once." She's right. Sears Tower. World Trade Centre. The Shard. The Burj. I've been up top on all of them. The view holds you for about a minute. These buildings must have been funded by a conspiracy of lift-manufacturers.

There's no revered tradition of Sufi mysticism in Dubai. No profound works of Muslim scholarship. No classics of Bedouin poetry. There is a Dubai Opera, but they don't have much opera in it. A layer of sunscreen is as about as deep as it gets here. Maybe some of the older Emiratis could give you a tip or two about fishing, but that's it.

Vikki returns her gaze to the menu. She always took a long time choosing. I study her choker. She got it from her grandmother. Silver, art whatever, with a distinctive heart-shape in the centre. From the nineteen-twenties, maybe older.

I wouldn't haven't recognized her at the art gallery without that. I didn't think oh, that's Vikki with her choker. I looked at her and thought that old trout has a choker, rather like Vikki's. It was only because the woman kept looking back at me, thinking that old git has a scar on his cheek, just like Dan's, that we figured it out. And that nose. Thirty something years.

Vikki couldn't wear that choker in London now. She was pushing her luck wearing it thirty years ago. When we went out, I was always primed to bash someone in the face if they tried to snatch it. She wore it a lot, even in bed. But, the irony about Dubai is that however many obesities of evil are loafing around, it's safe on the streets. Whatever gripes people have here about the city, and it does get hot and expensive, they all love the safety of their bling as they cavort about.

How they love long numbers in Dubai. Long numbers trooping into their banks and businesses. Counting in the counting-houses, gaining on the gains, however gotten. This is the place where you come when you need to put some distance between yourself and home, for whatever reason. Warlords, gangsters, fly-by-nighters, imaginative accountants, retired headmasters, *haramis* of all nations, they flock here. Some of them terrify me, but you don't have to worry.

Because the heavies, the top torturers are happy. They've been pacified. Pacified by retail ecstasy. Bling bliss. The happy don't cause trouble. Whatever they want, they can get. Shop till you drop. The cheese of their choice. Unlimited dream footwear. The armoured Bentley in a colour the factory would refuse to consider. Gucci body armour. Dorset crab or Wienerschnitzel. A slave. Or two.

The poor don't cause trouble either. The poor know their place. You're unlikely to be a victim of crime here, unless it's your other half stabbing you or doing a runner with the emeralds. Lack of democracy and shitty prisons have an upside. Shitty prisons where they don't reform but deform. But you still feel there's nothing holding up the scenery. I've been here two years, which makes me an elder, but I'm still visiting. I haven't invested. I rent a flat, because more so than in many other places, there's nothing holding up the scenery.

Vikki looks up from the menu. "You're having the crab, aren't you?"

I am having the crab. I've made my decision, because I know I'll live to eat another day. A Wienerschnitzel day will come. The waiter hovers close by. You better do something else, I think. Vikki continues to gaze at the menu. She'd read menus like they were novels. Thick ones. That hasn't changed.

I wonder if she's actually here. Is it really her? Why am I having lunch? I suggested lunch by reflex, because I didn't know what else to do. What do you say after thirty years? Somehow not suggesting something would have been a massive snub of our lives. I was expecting her to politely decline.

You have to say something when you haven't seen someone for thirty years. "And how was life?" Of course, now you can always go to the computer, click away and find out almost anything. I admit, late at night, a couple of times I looked for Vikki, found nothing, guessed she had changed her name, remarried, died, whatever, or was living without hitting a digital tripwire. It can be done.

"The duck please," Vikki finally announces. The waiter almost sighs with relief.

A strange thing has happened to me in the last few months. I can travel in time. Really. Amazing on the one hand, not so amazing on the other. I can't travel back to medieval London and go jousting. Or have a booze-up with Julius Caesar. I can only travel in my life. And I can't change anything. I can only go back and re-be. Oh, and I don't get any choice.

But it's not like a memory, where you keep a few moments, a few thin slices, a few details. A skeleton version. This is a super meaty memory with veg and trimmings, with everything. Loud and clear. All the unnecessary, uninteresting, squishy bits. Every item in the room, every crack in the wall, the dust on the windowsill, squeezing the last bit of shampoo out of the tube, a slight itch in your left nostril, a whiff of onion.

And it's not for the big events. Dull, unmemorable stuff. I find myself looking for a parking space or changing a tyre thirty, forty years ago. Brushing my teeth in March 79. I haven't told anyone, because it's so weird. I doubt anyone would understand or believe me. Maybe it's happened to others and they too kept quiet. Maybe it's outro stuff, the brain falling apart, or some tumour. I told the Doc I had some headaches. They did a scan. All good apparently.

There are probably only six or seven landmark conversations in your life. Let's say seven, because that's one of the power numbers. Crossroad conversations. Quite often, you only spot that years later. Many years later. I find myself reliving the moment Vikki told me about the dog.

It was a reverse charge phone call. From the USA. The cost still hurts. It was a different era.

"Have you been out, today?" I ask.

"No." Vikki was in the sunshine capital, Los Angeles, but she wouldn't leave her apartment for days.

"You should go out for a walk, even if it's only for five minutes."

"I know."

I observe a lone black sock on my worn carpet as Vikki tells me that she and Jasper are still arguing about custody of their dog, Zeno. I liked Zeno and I understand how close you can get to a dog, but that was the moment I realized it was over. Someone can say something quite trivial, but like the last number of a combination, it opens up a whole new perspective.

I realized that I was a spectator. A handyman. At best a volunteer therapist. A supplier of 'oh dears". Maybe a mug. All that.

I've known divorces so amicable it was hard to tell there was a divorce because all parties involved in the split were sleeping with each other, living with each other and collecting each other's dry cleaning for years afterwards.

Vikki's was the opposite. It was a masterpiece of acrimony. I can imagine it being taught in law schools. I'd listened to her complain about judges, lawyers, cleaners, dog-walkers, leaf-blowers, neighbours, the Livermore Lab, just about everyone she came into contact with in Los Angeles. If you want, you can spend your whole life in court.

Out there on her own in LA, she had a tough gig. One of the toughest. No family. No close friends. No serious back-up. No driving licence (although she was out there so long, she could have got one). It is amazing how much difference having a soul or two to say "oh dear" can make. But that was the moment I realized I didn't count. Or count enough. She was more invested in dispensing pain than in looking for pleasure. Or that her pleasure had become withholding a dog. That's what got her out of bed in the morning.

I doubt you can truly help anyone. You can encourage. You can lend a few quid. Give directions to the station. You can give useful tips about plumbing. There are two incurably sad things. You can't make someone like you, let alone love you. And you can't really help anyone, even if you want to. Not the big things. But I had done what I could. Vikki had promised that she would come back to London. And when I heard she and Jasper were going back to court over the dog, I knew I didn't matter. Or matter in the way I wanted to matter.

While I don't think you can help anyone in a life-changing way, I've done two major extractions from deeply deep shit. Some weighty aid. You lend someone ten quid or a shirt and they might be grateful. You pull someone right out of the shit when it's up to their nose, there's a good chance they'll hate you because you've seen them at rock bottom, seen their naked nakedness, and because they owe you big.

฿

"I almost didn't recognize you, you know," Vikki says.

"The choker was the giveaway for me."

"What a good memory you have. We should drink to Mandy for bringing us together."

Mandy, whose art gallery we met at, is an old friend of hers. I know Mandy because she's Ming's wife. Thanks to Ming's crypto gains, Mandy has the lolly to open an art gallery (maybe her Big Moment) and I had the obligation of attending the launch of a lot of purple paintings by someone Swedish (who must have got a hefty discount on a load of purple paint). I'd sooner be in a bath of acid than an art gallery, but you have your obligations, and you need to get out and about every day.

You wouldn't gather much about Vikki by observation. She still gives little away. Need-to-know basis. Some women you get their entire history over two cocktails, she's the very opposite. We're both sitting here opposite each other, cordially, as if making polite chit-chat about the weather in a dentist's waiting-room, but I used to tongue her bum. With gusto all round.

Vikki still has that stern senior librarian front. However, her breasts were so sensitive, you could practically make her come by staring at them. Her front is very stern. Am I looking at a husk? The dining dead?

"I thought of you, the other day, funnily enough," Vikki almost smiles. "I was watching, who was it, that band? Never mind, there was a drum solo, a long one, and I remembered what you said: 'All music is a drum solo.' That was your pithiest line."

I did say that. Because what happens in a drum solo? Loud. Soft. Fast. Slow. And those are the elements that make up all music. Mix them anyway you like. You always get gifted something by your friends, your intimates. It was Vikki that got me into the piano.

In solitude is how I like my music. Musicians must hate me because I want their best performance on digital and then they may withdraw. Haydn was someone's butler, wasn't he? Music must be the cruellest business. You can have no talent at all, you can pick up a guitar for the first time, make some noise, fart, and someone in Japan will rate you a genius. Or you can spend decades working the frets, shred it like Mr Hendrix, but you end up with three fans, and one will be your mum. On second thoughts, maybe it is like every business.

I never understood the charm of being deafened at a concert. If I want to be shoved and have beer poured on me, I can go to any pub, for free.

My brother took me to see David Bowie once, at the first of his last-ever shows, in Hammersmith. It was the night when he killed Iggy or whatever. Gary had a smudge of food dye on his face that made him look like an unemployable clown. It was some strange deal where my father told Gary he'd only get the money to buy a ticket if he took me. I can't remember if it was to punish Gary who had just liberated the bathroom basin from the wall, or whether it was meant to be some bonding ritual to keep us brothers tight.

I had just hospitalized Gary. We had been roughhousing at home, and he had been aiming to kick me in the balls, going for a real cobbler-crusher, but I slammed a door to block the kick. He started howling and rolling around on the ground and I didn't understand why. It was a while before the pain allowed him to mime that his fingers had been wedged in the door frame when I shut it. He had two broken fingers. My father commented: "Let's hope no one is sitting on our favourite bench at the hospital."

I left the concert after twenty minutes, because we were at the back, the sound was terrible, and I could hardly see anything. Gary wouldn't talk to me for a week. Music often ends up being your best friend, and you don't have to walk it like a dog, or deal with its turds. But not everyone can be your best friend.

"How have your friends fared?" Vikki asks. I'm surprised, because I did everything I could to keep my friends away from Vikki. It's odd what you remember. I certainly know that. Vikki pauses.

"Parrish?" she asks. "What happened to Parrish? And the martial arts fanatic?"

My friends? What a bunch. I don't think any of them got the Big Moment. Some had some good moments. Parrish ended up teaching English in Japan although his students had to, with extreme courtesy, suggest he was wrong about almost everything, even the spelling of cat. Not two t's. London variant, he explained. Only a real Londoner, a true geezer, a granite Cockney, would spell catt that way. Spelling it that way would make you fit in. Maybe he had a point. Some of the students thought it was drunken master, Zen mind tricks, deliberate mistakes to test them. It wasn't.

But Parrish was getting good money, and the young ladies queued up for a sample of hundred per cent unadulterated London cock.

"No joke. I'm not being funny, Dan. I'm at it so hard, Dan, I've had to stop. I'm terrified it'll fall off. It's looking awful. Like roadkill. No joke" He went to Bali for a week, flew back to Tokyo, found a sniffer dog next to him in the queue at immigration. In his right pocket was a flake of weed so tiny it was almost invisible to the naked eye. The arresting officer actually apologized: "This is the most embarrassing day of my career." But no more Japan for you, Parrish.

The Big Moment. Stu came close to the Big Moment. The at last. Stu had the blackest of black belts in Kyokushinkai. He took it so seriously. Insane burpees. Trained with the national team. He did mad stuff, like go for runs, barefoot, in the rain, at dawn. Ideally, you'd want an isolated, mossy cave with an icy stream to immerse yourself in, in solitary torture, for a taste of enlightenment, but you don't get many of them in Catford. I'm all for discipline but why not discipline around eleven o'clock when the sun is out, in comfortable shoes so you don't get bits of glass in your hoof? Maybe most practitioners of martial arts hope to one day put them to humanitarian use. Volunteer hero.

Stu confided in me that he hoped he could save some damsel from distress or protect some pensioner from muggers. Do some good. Make a Difference. Have the Big Moment. The show-stopper. Improve the world. Be seen. All that.

Stu came close. Once in the high street some half-naked giant, totally bug-eyed, was screaming and terrifying shoppers, waving a proper jungle machete around. I saw the photo in the local paper. I would have run a mile, shoving the distressed damsels out of the way.

Stu made the mistake of being reasonable. He gently asked the giant to put the machete down. To Stu's despair, the giant did exactly that and then spent an hour wailing how his wife had accidentally thrown his stamp collection out. It was the accidental bit that hurt the most. "I did her best friend. She didn't mind that much. The stamps were safe when I gave her friend a good seeing-to." Stu felt obliged to buy him a couple of pints and the giant invited him on a camping holiday in Wales.

"Parrish? Stu? They did okay," I reply. "I hear from them, time to time."

"Good," says Vikki. "I'm pleased. It's hard to get to the end without feeling a little cheated."

"Short-changed? I know what you mean."

"Have you been short-changed?"

"Hard to say. I've been lucky in some things. Very lucky. Unlucky in others."

"We all get a mixture, don't we?" Vikki adjusts her cutlery. "We don't get to choose the delivery dates. You lucked out with crypto?"

"Hard to say. I suppose I was."

Was I lucky? Well, you're in the lucky bracket if you're breathing. But I crawled. I crawled on all fours till my knees hurt. I dragged myself forward like a wounded soldier, swearing like one. I cried, I sobbed when some bags went down. I didn't shave for months so I could save on the foam and the blades. I looked like an abominable something. People crossed the street. I fasted for days. I scraped together every penny I could, to stick it into crypto. Getting packed for the banana zone. Lucky suggests there was no suffering.

"How's superluminous communication?" I ask.

That was Vikki's ambition, to make a mark in physics. To be a contender. Vikki had been trying to beat light. To outrun light, to go faster. To leave Einstein in the rearview mirror. Just overtake light, you overturn everything. All that. I didn't understand any of it, but it was apparently the biggest deal. I would have liked to help in some way because it meant so much to her, but all I could do was say good luck and offer lunch. We all have the plan. Or at least we all had the plan. It'd been a surprise to me that the career of science was as punishing, as bent as boxing. Who knows who. Some outright fraud.

"Doing very well without me," Vikki says.

Who's to blame? Who are the guilty ones? Who would you shoot first? The lawyers? The bankers? The therapists? The physics professors? Like fantasy football, late at night when I have trouble sleeping, I play fantasy executions. Obviously, the line-up changes over the years. It's harmless and it costs nothing. It takes a lot to actually do something.

One of the almost-big name tennis players I handled got a fat wad to play some sets with the smitten daughter of Ukrainian oligarch. She could barely return the ball, but my client had fun and ended up staying the night at the mansion outside Nice, partying and boozing.

In that early morning, in that 'you're my best mate, you are' window, he was embraced by the vodka-sodden Pops: "You've been so kind, let me do you a favour. Only one. No more. You get only one. Don't ask for more. No repeats. Okay? No repeats. But is there anyone you'd like to disappear? To visit the dark side of the moon? No stain, no problem at all for you, nothing on your shoe, no come back on you."

"I was tempted," my client told me. "But you know, you can't come back from there, can you? You can't edit that out. So the coach who dumped me from the national team? Almost finished my career. I gave that a lot of thought. But when I'm tired and down, I use that hate to power me up. Maybe I'll regret turning down the offer when I'm old and grey."

I did know someone who went as far as to hire a contract killer. Tree-hugger Trev. Honestly, one of the nicest guys I was at school with. I didn't hang around with him much because you don't want to hang around with the kids who are always getting beaten up, but he lived in the same street as me, and his sister was very generous with her time.

Trev opened a bike and skateboard café, with a used book section about growing dope, squatting, doing inspirational stuff with your turds. One thousand and one uses for a lentil. Design your own windmill. All that. Recycle, recycle, educate, educate. Trev wanted to change the world, but maybe Catford wasn't the place to start. They say it's changed.

Business was bad because there was a steady stream of people walking in, grabbing a bike, grabbing a skateboard, grabbing a cake, and here's the most incredible bit, even grabbing a book, and then walking out. Meandering out. Lighting a cig and meandering out. They didn't scarper and they didn't pay any attention to

Trev courteously explaining that what they were doing was bad for them, bad for the neighbourhood and bad for the planet. He lectured one or two all the way back to their homes. Trev was a model of persistence, but he never got an item back.

Not far from Trev's was a gun shop. Quite a famous one in South London. No one ever stole anything from them.

There's the old joke. How do you get a small fortune in investing? Start with a big one. Trev kept at it for years. His parents passed away and he sold their house to keep the café going and he made some money repairing bikes and giving classes in advanced compost-design. He worked his guts out, but you only had to take one look at him to see he didn't eat much.

I hadn't seen him for years when I spotted him on a park bench looking awful. That completely gutted stare. It took him a few moments to recognize me and although I didn't want to, I took him for a drink, because although I don't believe there's any reward for good behaviour, there is that slim chance you might get punished for wilful neglect. Sometimes you just can't walk by.

And did I want to. When someone's down, standard lines like chin up, tomorrow's another day, if you deliver them with enough insincerity, they can have a brief effect. But Trev was a mess. Ultrabankrupt, living on his sister's sofa, his last bike stolen. He was bitching about a partner who had cheated him, left him with huge debts, and worse, made him a radioactive outcast in the tree-hugging game. "Dan. I'd had enough. You might think less of me, but I decided he had to go, so I thought I'd go to a professional."

I did splutter into my pint when he said that. This from someone who wouldn't stop a ten-year-old walking off with a skateboard. I know I have a prominent scar, and I know that in the wimpy tennis management business I'm considered a hard case because most of them are wet tissues. I know that Trev and I go back a far way, but why are you telling me about murder?

"I hired a hitman," Trev said. Soon as he told me that I thought, right this has ended badly. The only hitman stories you hear about are married folk trying to get out of marriage by hiring an undercover policeman or a conman. If you want something done, do it yourself. There are no good stories, no happy endings as far as I'm aware of in any sentence with the word hitman in them.

"I had a friend in Serbia," Trev said. "I worked with him on a wetland reclamation project one summer, who complained a lot about his cousin, who was a nutter, who flew around Europe bumping people off. 'Terrible things happened during the Civil War,' he'd say. 'Awful, unbelievable things were done, things worse than killing. My cousin Boban did awful things to the enemy. He did awful things to his own side. He left school at fifteen, I have a doctorate, I work sixty hours a week, I can't afford a flat. Boban has a five-bedroom house with a swimming pool and a robot cleaner.'"

"Let me guess," I say. "It didn't work out."

"It was an awkward call," Trev continued. "Not a call you know how to make. Dragan, how are you? How's little Elena? Really? University already? The family? Well? Listen, small favour, could you put me in touch with your cousin Boban, you know the cousin, the one who travels a lot for business.' But he didn't mind."

Trev had got some money by putting in a grant in his sister's name from the National Lottery to help maintain the habitat of some endangered spiders in a quarry in Northumberland. "The spiders aren't going to grass me up, are they? I mean, I moved a couple of rocks. Took some pictures. Got volunteers from the British Arachnological Society to turn up. They're rock solid."

Trev met the hitman, who was fussy. He insisted on all the money up front. "Boban wanted references. He wanted to see a utility bill to see who he was dealing with. Took pictures of me. Showed me a short video about the possible consequences. It was like applying for a mortgage. Boban said he'd be back in a few weeks under a different identity to . . . er."

"And, let me take a wild guess here, that was the last you saw of Boban and your money, yeah?"

"Yes."

I nodded sympathetically. With real sympathy. We've all done stupid things. Investing in meme coins. "But it's not what you think. Boban didn't do a runner. You remember that civilian plane that was blown up over the Ukraine by the Russians?"

"Vaguely."

"Boban was on it, going to some job in Kuala Lumpur."

"No chance of a refund."

"No chance at all. But that's not the worst thing, Dan. The lottery people, out of the blue wanted to run a check on the project."

"But you said the spiders wouldn't grass."

"But I didn't want any trouble for my sister. She was applying for a massive grant, seeing how easily I had milked them, for a women's shelter."

"Do give her my regards."

"I will. I had to remove any debate about how they had been affected. I had to camp out for three days in that quarry to find those shifty little fuckers and stamp on them, to skew the data, so I could take pictures and claim vandals had stomped them."

I offer to buy Trev a couple of lottery tickets. "No. I've had my money, anyway. I don't want to squander any luck I have left on money." It was good he thought he had some luck left. That he had something coming to him.

฿

Everyone here in Dubai not an Emirati is visiting. This is a place that can't be home. Been here five years? You're visiting. It's like a party. You don't want to be there at the end, to round up the empties and scrape the vomit.

I stopped giving advice about crypto years ago, apart from the basics. Volatile. It's very volatile, and don't invest more than you can happily kiss goodbye. I often take a pause after saying it's very volatile, as if I'm thinking deeply and then I say it again. Double tap. But no one listens really.

What's the best-known fact about heroin? What's the one thing everyone but everyone knows, even eight-year-olds, about heroin? What's that word chained, glued, stapled, strapped, fucking ironed-on to heroin: addiction. That it's addictive. Has that ever stopped addiction? Or smoking. Verifiably bad for you, ridiculously expensive, stinky and smokers are still at it.

If there's one subject I know about, other than tennis, it's crypto. And the one thing that, like me, everyone who truly knows something about crypto will tell you is that no one knows anything about crypto. Someone somewhere said that. You only know that you don't know, if you're doing well. Attentive ignorance. Attentive ignorance. That's the best you can do.

Crypto? I can talk for hours. Coins. I can talk about them for hours. But what I'm talking about is the past, which is of limited benefit in dealing with the future.

How do you make money in crypto? The secret? You make money by losing money first. You get burned. Badly. Not flame-grilled. Bone-burning incineration. Rekt with chips. You can make money vanish in a completely irreversible way, like a conjuror. It's almost a mark of valour in crypto. "I was five million up and . . ." "I was ten million up and . . ."

Addiction gets a bad press. Rightly so because you can't call yourself an adult, you can't call yourself a man, you can't be admirable on even a small scale, even in the lower leagues, unless you have enough spine to deny yourself something. If you can't walk away. From booze, or gambling, or food, hot stone massages, nude sunbathing.

Okay we all have our support systems, our reward schedule,

our trusty sidekicks. Our favourite toy. Pacifier. Booze, food, coffee. I can't talk to anyone until I've had a coffee in the morning. But if you said to me, Dan, you don't have the bollocks to go without coffee for a year, I could do it because I'd have a reason to, although I wouldn't manage it in a dignified manner. I couldn't do it with a snap of the fingers and a smile.

Junkies, if they ever have any spare gear, like to offer it to others, to get them hooked. Not because they think they want to introduce others to the pleasure of dreamland, but because their lives would be easier if the whole world were hooked. But there are occasions when addiction can get you to somewhere you wouldn't have reached without it. Crypto was my addiction for a while. I did nothing else. There can be a fortune lurking in misfortune.

Vikki notices I'm tuned into the neighbouring conversation. Is it really her? It's as if an actress is playing her, flawlessly, the mannerisms, the delivery, but not her. Has she died? Is it the dining dead? Sometimes I wonder if I'm alive, because after all, I'm very much dead in so many ways. Vikki has great poise. the back is ramrod straight. Maybe that's because she likes to show the tits.

"You look well," she laughs. Is it the absurdity of it all?

"Thanks," I say. Just goes to show that you can fool even someone who knows you well. For a few hours at least. "So do you."

And Vikki does. It's not care, it's nature. Women often get rougher treatment. Many age like they trod on a landmine. Take Godiva. There wasn't a male at my school, and I'm including the teachers and the gays, and probably many of the girls, who didn't help themselves to Godiva in an imaginary way. She was unbearably dirty. Even now, thinking about her at school, my heart pumps up. We got on well, because I had no chance with her. No one at the school did. She had absolute power.

Every school has the prodigy, the fourteen-year-old who goes to nightclubs with twenty-year-olds and who has firm views on champagne. Her parents had given up, better that their daughter was spit-roasted by experts with bank accounts than knocked up by a dozy fifteen-year-old. Godiva brought us bulletins from the centre of London. I met her in a queue at the airport a while back. It was not only that I didn't recognize her. I didn't believe her.

"It's me, Dan, Godiva," she said and I almost said: "No, you're not." She had to repeat her name twice before the penny dropped. I couldn't believe it. It was like someone had painted her red and inflated her with a bicycle pump, and not in a good way. Even her earlobes had got bloated.

Vikki is a bit creased. You can't get away scot-free. But she has that steeliness. A peculiar, useless steeliness. If you or I turned up at an airport without a passport, we wouldn't get on the plane, no matter what we said, no matter how we argued or begged. If she turned up at the airport, and this did happen once, without a passport, somehow, she wangled herself through. In the end she was no better off than the people who remembered to bring their passport. She got the dog in the end.

Every day, luck is dished out. Good and bad. You don't get a say. That's the tricky question, better or not? Luck is dished out like grog. Sports management is a social business. Quite a bit of lubrication goes on. Champagne. Because champagne = success. Adding bubbles gives you success. Bubbles. Air. Oxygen. That's a metaphor. Or whatever. And although I'm not a big drinker you need a cocktail, because cocktails = sophistication. World traveller. Big spender. You're not a Millwall fan.

I nearly always order a Daiquiri, because that's something that's on every cocktail menu, and it saves you the trouble of reading about Mud Fight in a Church or Prime Minister's Pancreas or Gerbil Expectations, whatever outlandish name that some mixologist (mixologist = you pour alcohol out of a bottle into a glass) has come up with. And Daiquiri also opens up several well-trodden paths of small talk. Cuba. Thingamajig the writer. Grog, the British empire etc.

There are probably only half a dozen meals in your life that are really important. Landmark. Monument. Where you propose. Where you are offered the top job. Where you celebrate your son's degree. Where you're sacked.

The waiter pours mineral water into Vikki's glass, then my glass. Vikki waits for a moment to see whether I'm going for it, to see whether I'm wondering whether she remembers, then says: "Water is dangerous."

"Water is dangerous," I agree.

I told her that story. When I was fourteen, I woke up in the middle of the night, thirsty. I tiptoed down to the kitchen to get a glass of water. It was dark. I was sleepy and thinking a lot about Trev's sister, how generous she was, and I walked straight, slap-bang into the kitchen door, which for some reason had been closed. It was made of glass and cut my left cheek open. Right open.

There was a lot of blood, and embarrassment at the hospital, as no one at a hospital believes the walked-into-a-door story. I was dreading going to school.

"They're all going to laugh at me," I moaned to my father. My father had a look on his face that took me many, many years to recognize. It was the look of a father thinking: I'm giving it all I've got in the fathering department, and you go and do something like this.

"Here's an idea for you," my father said. "Don't tell them you walked into a door. Tell them you got into a fight with some bigger kids and they slashed you."

Like most brilliant ideas, it was simple. Lie. At school I told everyone I had got into it with some Millwall fans. It boosted my status permanently. I was now with the hard nuts. Not one of the top ones, because to get formally ranked you actually had to do someone hard in the playground, in a public and verifiable way, for everyone's entertainment, but a prospective hard nut.

I found myself saying hello to the hard nuts, getting nods in the street, which I didn't before. You obviously were going to get the worst of it fighting some Millwall fans, and somehow carrying a scar suggested you were tasty. The two great achievements of my school years were walking into a door and getting off at the school disco with the girl unanimously voted as having the best tits, which happened because I was standing next to her and she was drunk.

Vikki cuts into her duck breast, pins a slice onto her fork, assesses the colour, puts it in her mouth, starts chewing. She was serious about her food, she had lots of weird kitchen utensils I never found out did what, doing stuff with rowanberries. I'd never heard of a rowanberry until I met her, and despite her influence I never got past throwing something into a frying pan and letting it fry. And I'm still alive.

"Dan, do you think I was wrong to go to LA?"

Vikki's question is a questionnaire on my life. Give it marks out of ten.

Of course you were wrong. It ruined everything. It turned you into a pill-popper. Why are you asking this now? Now? But why say I was right? Why say I told you so? Being right is of no value in a firm or a marriage, or probably anywhere. Being an adult, or being a man, having wisdom, however you want to put it, means you swallow it. You pass up the easy hits. Because they can't do any good. There's nothing great about being a leader, on however small a scale. Considering others. What's the thing doctors swear? Do no damage? That's wonderful if you can figure out what does damage.

I begged Vikki not to go to LA when Jasper got some deal out there. Her relationship was, on casual inspection, at rock bottom. When your other half disappears for five days? Of course, it's not for outsiders to judge. But still, that's a low point. I begged her to come back. I did a lot of business in LA, some I needed to, a lot that I didn't need to do. There were murmurings at the firm.

What else is there but love? That's why people get married three, four or five times, even though they've probably missed the boat. Great to have some gongs, some applause, great to have big bags, plenty of space to park your collection of vintage motorbikes, but all that finally counts is company. Friendship's good, but love is great. You can plan some things, to some extent, you can't plan love.

"No," I say. "Of course not."

In blockchain there's the trilemma. Scalability. Security. Decentralisation. It turns out, you can't have all three full-on. One has to limp behind. I've noticed that elsewhere. In every trinity, there's a weak partner. Power. Truth. Love. If God were to whisper the answer in your ear, what would it be?

Do you need power if you have the truth? Do you need the truth if you have power? Do you need power if you have love? Most of us would go for love, but love on its own while if you had to choose one, is the one you'd go for, practically isn't enough. Company. Company is the great game. Although you don't get to choose who's in the room.

Love provides the best company, but if you don't have a job, if you don't have money, if you can't look after your wife or child, or help your stone china, love and loyalty can take a beating.

Vikki forks the last piece of potato from her plate. "The world is a fireball," she announces. "It's a cleverly disguised . . . unfireball-like fireball. But it's a fireball." Then laughs. If it's a joke, I don't get it. Perhaps it's some philosophical reference by some pusher of profundity. "Dan, you should know that. I'm a physicist remember. I promise you the whole world is on fire, you just can't see it, because you're so used to it."

"Did you ever remarry?" I ask. I realize I'm not interested, but I'm running out of conversation. She's better at silence. She nods.

"And?"

"It's not interesting. Marriage is marriage. You must know that."

That's all I'm going to get. She should have been a poker player. Nothing is given away. She can talk, but you find out nothing. The shield is up most of the time, and only comes off, briefly, with the clothes.

I only found out from her best friend that her father died when she was eleven, and the best friend only knew that since she had known Vikki since she was six. And Vikki was miffed that had slipped out.

Late at night, I doubt she looked me up. Vikki's tough. That's one of the qualities that made her attractive. She's tough and she's doesn't look back. Women make a lot of noise about emotions and getting worked up over mice in the kitchen, but it's a front. You can't be a good mother unless you're ruthless, willing to execute the prisoners. Tougher than me, because although I don't want to, I do look back. Tough, but crazy. Crazy before the therapists got to her, much crazier after.

We were in a hotel once in the US and Vikki accused me of being too tame. "You're such a rule follower." Me? The hotel floor we were on made a big circuit, you could walk around, pick up some ice from the ice machine, and get back to your room from the other side. She said I was too chicken to run the circuit naked. This coming from someone who grew up in Cheltenham. Cheltenham? A day in Catford is a year in Cheltenham. I might have lied about the Millwall scar, but there was plenty of other action. I should have medals for surviving. I didn't want to do the run because you don't know the levels in another country. Will people guffaw at my arse or call the police?

"You first," I said. So, she did. Ran out naked, picked up some ice, got back. Empty corridor. It was nearly a minute. It was a different era, and it was a cheap hotel so I don't think they had cameras, but that wouldn't have deterred her. Then I had no choice.

Half-way round, a guy in suit and tie, spotted me. "Is there a fire?'

"No," I replied, hoping he wouldn't see which room I was in.

฿

"It's an unapologetic watch," the crypto salesman is now talking about his watch. Unapologetic? An unapologetic watch? A watch that doesn't back down, or deny its watchness? You're forced to say some strange things to survive, but there's no excuse for this. I was willing to give him the benefit of the doubt, but this is tragic.

"Because I was undiagnosed," a girl about eighteen is saying four tables over. Four tables over. "In my defence, it wasn't my fault." Maybe it is her fault, for being so loud, so positively preachy. Hers is not a conversation, it's a performance. You don't have to inflict yourself on the whole restaurant. You really don't.

"Once I understood I had bulimia," she continues, "things were a little better, but of course, I discovered, talking to the helpline, I had everything, I discovered, you know, the autism, the Asperger's, I had to take the whole shop. I had to educate my mother about all that. It was very difficult to educate my mother about it. I get that from my mother, once I understood that . . ."

There seems to be a whole generation that collects conditions, sick notes like merit badges. Bulimia, depression, dyslexia, autism, whateverism. You're nothing unless you have some condition, which of course you're coping with, heroically, through incredible personal development and raw bravery. The occasional prescription. Cachet. Style and fashion.

Ms Diagnosed is the same loudmouth from my youth, she even looks the same. She's a loudmouth, just loud with a different pitch. Change. The opinions change, she stays the same. Now yum-yum. Then yuck. Then yum-yum. Now yuck. Now she has ailments for status. For bangles.

I don't understand how we managed to get out of trees, out of the caves, into cities, the journey from campfires to restaurants. How did we get to a crisp, spotless tablecloth and serving Dorset crab? How was that achieved? Who by? There seems to be no common sense, or any sense left. Has it simply evaporated? Where do the ideas come from? The momentum? The more you consider it, the theory that aliens turned up to impose civilization on us sounds plausible. I don't see how we could have made it this far on our own.

I pay the bill. Lunch was my suggestion after all. I give Vikki a farewell peck on the cheek. What else? It seems the thing to do. Like a distant relative. I look back as we part to see if she's looking back. She isn't. I'm not bothered. I'm glad lunch is over.

Two months later I get a call. "Is it that Dan? My name is Artemis. I've just arrived in Dubai. My mother said I should give you a call. I'm Vikki's daughter."

I FOLLOWED A small ball. For a long time. Long before Bitcoin.

No one in Catford played tennis. I only got a racket because a friend was moving to Taiwan and the family dumped nearly everything for the move. Everyone played football. There was swimming. No one played tennis. Carrying a racket was like carrying a sign: beat me up, punch me in the face, please. That was probably the attraction for me. It was a sort of rebellion. A sneer to my surroundings. That you were on your own was an attraction. Not a team game. "You should play a team game," my father said to me." It teaches you how to work with others, and how to lose."

"I don't want to learn how to lose," I said. I definitely had the attitude. I believed I could go all the way.

It was hard. Tennis requires money in a way that football doesn't. You can always hit a ball against a wall, and I did, for hours. You can play at Wimbledon in a pink jockstrap now, but then clubs had strict dress codes. It was a different era. Money, money, money. We just didn't have the money for the good tennis club. Or any tennis club. Or coaching.

I couldn't afford to join a club, but my Big Cousin solved the problem. "Here's the trick. You don't pay them. They pay you."

"How?"

"Get a job, you twat."

"How?"

"Don't ask for a job, tell them they need to give you a job. Go in there, and don't leave. Just don't leave. When they tell you it's no use waiting, you don't leave. You don't leave till they switch off the lights. And lock the doors. You don't leave until you've talked to everyone at the club. At least twice. Volunteer to empty the bins or sweep up. Just start doing it. Go to the shops for biscuits. Collect balls. Whatever. When they say, we can't pay you. You say well I'm willing to work for membership. Be a massive nuisance. Be such a nuisance that they'll agree to just about anything just to get rid of you. You go in and you say to yourself I'm not leaving until I've got a job or membership. I don't care if it takes eight hours and I don't eat. Look pathetic and sad. They'll feel sorry for you or they'll want to shut you up. Both work."

Many years later I realized that my Big Cousin knew that being a nuisance or harping on sympathy was no guarantee of getting a foothold. Nothing guarantees anything. He was just turbo-charging me, brain-pumping me to have a good crack. He sounded so convincing. I believed him. It sounded like the truth. It worked. I think they were sorry for me. I helped out at weekends, evenings and holidays, and even worked on the bar. Really, I'd be nowhere without booze and drugs.

Monstro.

I left school at sixteen. For two years, I did nothing but tennis.

I can tell you the exact moment I called it quits. Half-past-three on a Saturday. I was beaten at my club, by a girl. It wasn't that I was beaten. Or beaten badly. Or that it was by a girl. It was that I was outclassed. She was thirteen, five years younger than me, and to make it worse, looked about eleven. She had just joined the club, everyone said she was star material. So small and skinny, she looked as if she would barely hold the racket. Her arms were chopsticks. She hit the ball so hard, I could rarely return it. It wasn't even so much the placing, which was perfect, but it was the power. It was like your racket hitting a wall. She could hit the ball that hard. It had been brewing for some time, but this was the moment I accepted there was no hope.

Reading the game is an important part of success, but that you can learn. That can develop. That comes with experience. That there was a gulf, a biological chasm between me and the pros, even the low-ranking ones was the shock. No amount of push-ups or weights or coaching would change that. Muscle make-up, agility, hand-eye coordination, I don't know what it is, but I didn't have it.

I didn't think about working as a coach or club pro. I could have made it at that level if I'd wanted to, but my heart wasn't in it. That's the worst thing, no hope. When you know there's no hope. If I didn't have chance of getting to the top, however distant. Why? If you can't even buy the lottery ticket.

One afternoon can completely turn your world upside down. Kev, one of the most precocious muggers at my school, went into a local florist with a knife. The florist beat him up. She wasn't some broad-shouldered bull dyke. She was small. She didn't do martial arts. Her dad wasn't a boxer who'd shown her a few moves.

She was a small sixteen-year-old florist. Who punched Kev in the face once. He hadn't been expecting that. She smacked him in the mouth him again and he went down. Then she followed up with the boot. On his cobblers. A real cobbler-crusher. When the police arrived, he couldn't stand up. It was a different era. There was no CCTV or phone footage.

So, it could have been kept quiet. No one would have known about it, but Kev had invited two friends along to pretend to be customers and to watch him in action. The two friends didn't like Kev, because no one did, and it was all over Catford within an hour. My Big Cousin who was at the Police Station said he'd never seen coppers laughing like that. They put a begonia in his cell. Kev died as such. Better off dead. Counted out on the mugging. Catastrophe in a florist's. He left London. Decades later I heard, someone with his name, some reincarnation worked as a prison officer in Scotland.

B

I drifted a bit after waving farewell to tennis. But there were other activities.

I was waiting in the Green Man for a date who was already very late. I had met her at a club, where I had only got in because my Big Cousin was working on the door. I didn't have the money otherwise.

This is how young I was. First time I looked around the club, I dissolved in the music. I saw women in skimpy clothes. I smelled the shampoo, the moisturizers, the lip gloss, the soap, the perfume, the deodorant. All that.

Flesh and fragrance battered me. And this thought genuinely passed through my sixteen-year-old mind. This is paradise. I thought that. This is where they've been hiding it. Ha-ha, I've made it. I've won.

It took a while to learn that clubs are the worst place for picking up women, and especially if you get into dancing. Dancing was escape. I went with Parrish. He didn't dance unless forced to. I don't know whether being fit from tennis made me a good dancer (it's all in the toes) but it came naturally to me. Parrish would be trying to strike up conversations (almost impossible in a club) while I danced. And the more you danced, the less you cared about meeting women, the less you cared about anything.

One night I came off the dance floor, drenched in sweat and an attractive girl said to me, "You've been dancing." Not the wittiest line heard in a club, but no worse than many I've used. I got the message. We agreed to meet in The Green Man, the one pub we both knew.

I was waiting for my date in The Green Man. Like most boozers in London at the time it was smoky, stinky. Shitty, in short. Was there a place with a more romantic atmosphere in Catford? No.

A weedy punk walked past me and sat at a table opposite. He wore a black leather jacket that was much too big. He looked like a tent with one pole. "People = shit" was painted on the back of the jacket, clumsily, of course. In uneven, but very large letters. Not entirely inaccurate. He had a point.

We were well past the pogoing novelty of punk, so he didn't even have the virtue of being on the cutting edge. Jump on the bandwagon at the right time, pal. People = shit. A bold statement anywhere. A very bold statement in Catford when you're a weedy punk with specs. An insane statement in the Green Man. I was worried that he was sitting far too close to me, and that when they got round to kicking his head in, I'd get dragged into the ruck.

My date was forty minutes late, so the fear of being stood up loomed. That wasn't too bad a prospect, because I hadn't told anyone about the date. I hadn't told anyone in case I was stood up. Had I misunderstood something? Was there another Green Man in the area I didn't know about? We had said Tuesday at seven, hadn't we? It was a different era. Back then, mobile phones only existed in sci-fi films. I had a number for her, and there was a payphone, but it didn't work. I had to sit and wait. About another twenty years for mobile phones. What's it like for the kids now, when it's impossible to lose touch with anyone? How does that work? Back then, someone would move two miles away and you'd never see them again.

Misunderstandings. Misunderstandings. Misunderstandings and events, weather, they run everything. Weather and Misunderstandings. Pushing when you should be pulling. Pulling when pushing. Misjudgements. Missteps. Mishearings. Mistranslations. Misfirings. Mishaps. Mischief. A whole lot of missing going on.

I was stuck. I had no choice but to wait for my date and the arrival of mobile phones. I was also worried that my date would arrive as the punk was getting his kicking, which might kibosh any romantic prospects. I also needed a piss.

There was a problem. There were six Millwall fans on the side of the bar where the Gents was located, almost blocking the entrance. They were loud. Of course. They were throwing their presence about. Of course they were.

"I didn't want any trouble, so I stabbed him," one was cackling. "And my blade broke. I said to him, you're in real trouble now, sunshine, you've gone and done it now, you've broken my favourite knife."

To get into the Gents you had to squeeze past them. Really squeeze past them. Brush past them, pretty much. Six of them. Hazardous. As I considered relieving myself, it was noticeable how no one was visiting the Gents.

There's a lot of nonsense about how football hooligans were some sort of street athletes. With some warrior code of ethics. No civilians, no women, no kids stuff. All the keen boot-boys I knew were the worst sort of cowardly back-stabbing shits, like Kev, who'd only have a go if they had, say five friends with them and you weren't looking.

Back then, the Millwall fans were the worst. There were all sorts of stories. Some were true but served with a large dollop of bollocks. Like the Silver Spooner, for instance. The Silver Spooner, a supposed fan who brandished a silver spoon to gouge out the eyeballs of rival fans. Did he exist? Did he actually carry a spoon? Was it solid silver? Had anyone checked? If all those conditions were met, had he ever scooped out a single eyeball? From someone who wasn't a pensioner or a ten-year-old?

Going to the Gents would get me noticed. To make it worse, I was wearing my best outfit. If I'd been in labouring gear, covered in shit, I probably could have got away with it. I worked on a building site for a while and it was noticeable that if you walked around with a tennis racket, you got a lot of friction in Catford, but if you had filthy clothes, dirt in your hair and heavy boots, the respect was lush.

I did think about popping outside for a slash. Not unusual to see gentlemen pissing against a wall, a car, a church in Catford, but I imagined my date turning up just as I was taking my ease. Besides, I didn't want to feel I'd lost my bottle.

I tried to make myself as thin as possible. The second I got into the Millwall zone, one of them, clutching his pint, took a step backwards to give more room to another hilarious anecdote, perhaps about the Silver Spooner.

In an instant, your brain can process so much. I thought, well, now if you take a step backwards, without looking, that's your fault, not mine, for bumping into me and spilling your pint. I also contemplated that it would be no use in explaining that reasonable observation to a Millwall fan. That's the last thing I remember.

I came to, outside the Green Man, in the car park, in a puddle.

Was the puddle meant as a refreshing treat? My left ear hurt badly. My right eye was so swollen so I could barely see. I was covered in blood. My date never turned up, or perhaps she did as I was being dragged out. Well, finally I have been beaten up by Millwall fans. I can fully enjoy that glory. I got up and pissed against a wall. I never went back to the Green Man.

The most significant thing though was what happened between the loo and the car park.

I was somewhere safe. Somewhere far away. Somewhere comfortable. Like a giant womb. Dan? Dan was a flake of skin, a flake of memories. A very small, thin flake of skin I had shed. Gone. A mere toenail cutting, nothing much to do with me, and Dan's disappearance down the drain wouldn't matter. I was something bigger, somewhere else.

That's the question if this was some insight, and I've never told anyone about it, what are we doing here? If the total of Dan is almost nothing, two or three atoms more than a complete void, what's Dan doing here? What's the point of sitting through geometry lessons, waiting for buses, brushing your teeth? If, when we look straight at the night sky, see as far as we can see in the night sky, this is the just the doll's house, a small theatre or club, a stopover, why bother?

When I got home, I realized my watch was running more than an hour slow.

You don't realize what you're doing even on the small scale, let alone the intergalactic.

Me and my friend Joey, we went to Brixton. My Big Cousin had tipped me off there was a reggae single in Desmond's that Joey had been desperate to get hold of. "Do More Reggae" or "Reggae's really Reggae", some bollocks like that. I say my friend, but Joey was so friendly, could you say he was really friends with anyone? Shouldn't friendship involve some exclusivity? Some vetting? Guest list? A velvet rope, however invisible? That you're friends with some, but not with others. Joey was the class clown, but the sort of class clown that even teachers appreciated. The jokes were on him. He was so cheerful, it was immoral.

As we walked down Coldharbour Lane, a vast black woman, who must have been a distant aunt of Joey stopped us.

"Is that little Joey Ferron?" Joey, not that little, admitted it. The aunt interrogated him about fugitive nephews, the state of ackee fish etc.

"Are you happy in this country, Joey?"

"Yes, I am. I think I'd be happy anywhere." I realized he would be. He was a freak. Immune to pessimism. Doubt. Moaning. It was pissing with rain once, and he was getting soaked, but he was laughing. Just immune. I don't know whether Joey became a ticket inspector or the owner of a chain of supermarkets. He had already won. Hit the jackpot, the fucker. I envied him.

We all benefit from happy souls. The terrorists, the bomb-makers, the thugs, the Kevs, they're always miserable sods. I suppose

I can remember Joey saying how happy he was, and how unusual that conviction was, because some two minutes later the first Brixton riot started. The rioters were mostly much older than us. We watched a car being overturned. One guy started squirting some liquid on it, lighter fuel? He fished in his pockets, then turned to us: "Got a light?"

I always carried matches. I never smoked, but what if a girl asked for a light? If you didn't carry smoking paraphernalia, then you were severely limiting your prospects. Fire was a great ice-breaker.

I handed over my matches. The guy ignited the fluid and returned the box. That burning car I think was the first burning car of the riot, and pictures of it were used everywhere. Joey never behaved quite the same way towards me after that.

฿

But the small ball reappeared.

How did I get something that looked like a career? Parrish helped to change a spare tyre. He might not have done so if the car hadn't belonged to an attractive woman. Who had a friend, Sophie. Sophie forgave me for knowing Parrish and went out with me for a while.

Sophie had a flatmate at the time. I turned up for a weekend, and her flatmate Dimitri, whom I had only met once before, was in his dressing-gown, sneezing and coughing in a disgusting way.

"You know about tennis, right?" he rasped. Then he curled up in a bout of vicious coughing.

It was true. I had lost matches all over the country. Tournaments need losers. In fact, they need them much more than winners. You only need one winner, but a galore of losers. I had contacts all over the place. Dimitri worked for a sports management company and was supposed to usher some Paraguayan player around for the weekend. He begged me to stand in for him for a few quid.

So, we drove around for three days, trying to wildcard her into some tournament, because whatever organizers pretend, if you turn up with a racket and they have a gap because someone's pulled out, or their flight was cancelled, you get to play. Lourdes had fantastic breasts and surely I couldn't be churlish if she had a sexual emergency? But we didn't get a game and after seventy-two hours, mostly in a small car, eating sausage rolls at service stations, the atmosphere was tense.

Dimitri was grateful to me. "Her aunt knows someone who knows my boss. It was important she got shunted around."

I owe my career in sports management to Dimitri, or as he was shortly referred to afterwards, Disaster Dimitri. Not many people in Britain have heard of the domestic flight that crashed in 2002 in Brazil. Only a few of the passengers walked away from that one. Dimitri was one. You might remember the volcano eruption in New Zealand. That got some coverage. I saw pictures of Dimitri covered in ash. The terrible Indian Ocean Tsunami? Everyone knows that. Dimitri was at a café on the beach.

These are the ones I know about. I haven't conducted a thorough search.

Three weeks after my guided tour for the Paraguayan, Dimitri was in a car with the two rising stars of his sports management firm. One, who was the son of the boss's next-door neighbour and the other a clown who claimed to know Jimmy Connors's sister, and to have regular saunas with Borg's carpenter.

Dimitri wasn't driving. He was in the back seat when the car sped into a roundabout (usually easy to spot), took off, landed on its roof and killed the two rising stars in front. Practically the entire arse-licking department of the firm had been wiped out in one swoop. As a result, Dimitri was bumped up and needed to hire some support quick. I got the job.

Three weeks later, the company office was burgled. Cleaned out. They even took some light bulbs. Maybe it was a joke. The good news was that the fire that destroyed the office two weeks after that didn't matter so much. Our chief accountant fell into a mysterious coma that lasted for two years and that no one could explain.

Dimitri left the company. I was hoping for elevation of course, it seemed natural that my career should be meteoric, but the boss's neighbour had a distant nephew who was brought in. Dimitri had gone to work for our main competitor, who about six months later went bankrupt, not long after their founder was killed by a golf ball (while playing with Dimitri). Dimitri left the country and I lost touch with him (something very easy to do at the time). It was a different era.

But I heard things. Usually long after the event. But I heard things. As far as I know, his plane was only hijacked once. He was at a beachfront hotel when the tsunami hit. Not everyone died. He was in Kuwait when the Iraqis invaded, and was heavily shelled in Georgia when he was planning on investing in their wine, apparently excellent. A Tuscan retreat was marred by his entering his room and discovering a dead chamber maid. He was in a little-known coach crash in Bulgaria which killed a couple of dozen.

You don't want to believe in a jinx, but facts are facts. The Wheel is the Wheel. Sometimes the Wheel just stops. Does he somehow generate disaster or is it just some intergalactic curse that makes him a beacon of misery all the time?

I once bumped into him in Old Compton Street and he wanted to go for a drink. Dimitri was always friendly to me, but let me be frank, I was too scared. I felt ridiculous and ashamed of my cowardice. Every man wants to feel a bit special forces. No one wants to bottle it, or at least to be seen bottling it. Or to feel as if you're bottling it.

Dimitri had bought a place in the country and a mutual friend had recently gone to visit him. He knew Dimitri's reputation but had felt it was too much to blank him. Every man wants to feel a bit special forces. Backing out wasn't special forces. His wife begged him not to go. "He's got a cottage in the Kent countryside. The real only danger is being bored to death applauding the village cricket side," he argued. "What else could happen? My jugular ripped out by a shirty hedgehog?" He disappeared into a cesspit in Dimitri's garden. He managed to walk again after six months or so.

When I came across him in Old Compton Street, I thought Dimitri'd be pale and worn down by all the misery, but he had put on a bit of weight and was jolly. It's like with four-year-olds, whatever your life is, you think it's normal.

I was just too scared to go for a drink with Dimitri. There was no upside to having a drink. The best outcome was not dying or going to intensive care. The great thing about having kids is that they provide ready excuses for getting out of things. You sigh. "I'd love to, but my son . . ."

The nail-bomb went off in the Admiral Duncan an hour later. Dimitri helped the wounded out.

฿

But Dimitri got me in. Parrish changed the tyre, but Dimitri opened the door. I realized that I was a good employee, not because I was cleverer (although I usually was) but because I was willing to work harder. Or actually work. I was usually first in, and last out. I was excited by the prospect of a career. Unlike the odd jobs I'd been doing selling booze and drugs. The firm did mostly tennis, but other sports, football, boxing. I got to travel. I travelled abroad for the first time when I was twenty-one. I shook hands with Pele.

When, in recognition of the lunatic hours I worked, they

said I could hire an assistant I felt like a narco baron. A major supervillain. Now you'd just use your phone. Interviewing was depressing because you saw good candidates who badly wanted a job, but you could only hire one. I gave the job to a sparky girl who had trained as a bullfighter for a few months, who spoke Spanish and French fluently and insisted sports management was her dream. She didn't turn up on the Monday morning she was supposed to start. Or any other day. Maybe she was kidnapped by aliens.

Then my boss intervened. He knew a perfect candidate. Gina, the daughter of a friend of his. This seemed like trouble. Danger. No-win situation. I was already working on my grand philosophy, never put yourself into a shaftee posture, then you can't get shafted. It's obvious in a way, but genius nevertheless. The only flaw in this very sound philosophy is that the only way to have a surefire way of avoiding the shaftee posture is to stay at home, hiding under your bed.

When Gina did turn up, two minutes early on Monday morning for work, I was hugely relieved. She got me a coffee, and I spent much of the day reflecting on how I didn't need an assistant. I spent almost as much time explaining a task to her as it would have taken for me to do it myself. But an assistant. It was the start of an empire.

Tuesday, Gina didn't turn up and since I was so busy, I assumed she'd had some unexpected crisis. Boiler. Relative in hospital. I wasn't bothered because I was up to my ears. Wednesday afternoon when she was still absent, and no one had seen her, I talked to her mother who said she wasn't at home but that she'd pass on my message. I got a call a few hours later.

"Gina, how are you? I was wondering where you are?"

"I'm in Ibiza."

I was confused. Was this some club, restaurant, swish hairdressers or trendy boutique I didn't know about?

"What's Ibiza?"

"You know, the island. In the Med."

"Why?'

"I'm on holiday. I'm having a fantastic time here. You said I was entitled to three weeks."

I had said that. She was entitled to three weeks' holiday. I don't think Gina was trying it on. She was so out to lunch, so involved with herself, that it hadn't occurred to her that she should mention going on holiday to someone at the firm, let alone me or that some paperwork might be involved or that shooting off on the second day of your job was in some way wrong.

My Big Cousin had said to me. "When there's a problem, when it goes pear-shaped, stay calm. Anyone can lose their temper, yeah? It's not an achievement. Anyone can shout, anyone can swing a punch. What you need to do is look around. You need to look for the advantage. What's the best solution for you? Where's the road out of Shit City? Sometimes, there isn't one. But you should look for it. If a punch in the mouth is required, you always have that option later on."

It's one of the proudest moments of my life that I didn't blow up. I was lucky it was a phone call. My face would have betrayed me. I was brilliant. I was so cool. I even wished her a good time. In a sincere tone. But there was worse to come.

How tight was her mother with the boss? The boss was one of these irritating rich gits who dress badly and carry everything in plastic bags. You wouldn't want to sit opposite him at a dinner table. The story was he had conned a big loan from some simpleton at a bank and set up the sports management company without so much as a tired masseur on the books. And no interest in sport of any kind.

He knew no one in tennis or any sport. He rented an office. Placed some ads. Built an athlete-trap, and they walked in. Later on, when I discussed him with others in the business, they all talked about him with a mixture of fantastic hatred and admiration.

The only subject that he spoke about with any enthusiasm was bollards. That's right, those small posts, blocking access. He was into bollards and was a member of the international bollard appreciation society. That definitely existed. I checked up on that. He once showed me some pictures of some fancy wrought-iron bollards in Paraguay. I didn't know how to arrange my face. Was it a test? Poker face? I crafted a look of mild pleasure which could be interpreted as quiet mirth, in case he was winding me up.

For years, when I travelled round on business, I'd send him pictures of intriguing bollards from around the world. Beverly Hills, Versailles, Soweto. I'd always get an appreciative response. For years I was convinced it was a long-game wind-up, a joke, and that one day, he'd burst out laughing and denounce me as a dickhead for believing him. It never happened.

But the bollard-spotter, he had a major international company. Despite not caring about sports or doing any work. I still lived with my parents. I wouldn't have lasted at the company but for the de facto boss, the one who came into the office and did the work, Rosamund.

She sounded like was from some film in the 1930s, and should have been in an old-people's home. She had to be seventy plus. Someone from another world, not just a post code. Rosamund had played at Wimbledon in that time, when if you rolled up at Wimbledon with the correct apparel, you could play at Wimbledon. She was an aristo from a boarding school where they worried about French verbs or what the German was for elderflower. At my school we concentrated on finding innovative ways to burn down classrooms. We shouldn't have got on, but we did. You never know. Everyone needs a backer. Ideally, half-a-dozen.

You never know. Stu got a job in the mailroom of a big ad company in Soho. The first morning he was asked to park the boss's car in the underground garage. Top-of-the-range Merc, that was no longer top-of-the-range after Stu reversed it hard into a concrete pillar. He wasn't fired, he ended up with a career in ads, although he hated it. "Writing off the boss's car got me noticed."

When something disastrous has happened at work, the only question you need to ask is who knows? Can this be buried? Will the coverup make it worse? As it usually does.

฿

The players only had one obsession. How do I get better? You weren't on the circuit unless you were solid, your serve faster than a speeding bullet etc. But how do you get better?

They say you are your own worst enemy. But your worst enemy has many, many allies. Someone said so, somewhere, sometime. Your laziness. Your temper. Your love of pizza. And in pro tennis you are truly playing yourself again and again. Different shapes and sizes, but versions of you.

You're looking at you. Someone who's fit. Tough. Motivated. Someone just like you. Someone who hasn't come to lose. Someone willing to sweat for three hours to win a single point. Someone waiting for you to pull a muscle, to pick up a bug at an airport, to have a blazing row with your partner or coach or accountant. To fall apart somehow. To have a chink.

So how do you get more unplayable serves? How do you perfect line-hugging backhands? How do you improve at that level? The answer? No one knows.

But you can make money making up answers. Towel bicep curls? More broccoli? Less broccoli? Poetry? Weights? Drugs? Siesta? Sex, more or less? Learning the banjo? More broccoli? Purple potatoes? Black tomatoes? Some religion that hasn't been practiced since the Romans gave it up? Yoga in the rain? Different drugs? What will give you that edge to sneak past your competitors? And as you get older, how do you even keep up?

I only have to watch you hit balls for three minutes, no more. I know whether you're simply sporty, or well deadly. Talent spotting isn't hard. It isn't. Talent couldn't be more obvious. If you're asking the question, does this player have it? The answer is no. Locating the talent in the first place, that's another matter. I never had anything to do with coaching, thank God. Managing the players was draining enough.

฿

The boss? I never chatted much with the boss. He didn't come into the office much, and when he did, with his plastic bag, a plastic bag that had seen plenty of action, not a plastic bag from a chic boutique or fashionable destination, he didn't talk much.

Sporadically, he'd notice you and say: "Are you working?". If you weren't in the office, you'd get the same message two or three times a year: "Are you working?" This wasn't some running joke. Or curiosity about your activities. He didn't do jokes. This was his management technique, and it worked. The firm did well.

He once showed me pictures of the bespoke bollards outside his Cornish getaway. I didn't pay much attention to the bollards. I did to his six-bedroom waterside mansion. And the moored boat. The firm didn't have what you'd call global clout, but it worked. It was so wrong.

He saw us as stress druids. That was the only remark that came out of his mouth about our work. "We're stress druids." It's pithy. Colourful. I always liked that term. I can't believe the boss came up with it. He wasn't Welsh. He must have heard it somewhere. And it was true. Most of our work was lifting some of the stress off the backs of our clients. Telling them that they were wonderful. Booking hotels. Filling in tax forms and visas. Doing accounts. When I started, if you wanted the accounts done airtight, you got some Chinese woman to do it. It was a different era. After 2,000 or so, we started abandoning the Chinese, because software and dozy interns could sort it out.

Everyone's supposed to have a secret. If I have a secret, it's that I don't have one. It's all out there my life. No unacknowledged kids. No spicy criminal convictions. I never murdered Jasper. None of that.

Everyone is supposed to have the plot that failed. The mission that turned out to be impossible. Wanting to make it as a tennis player was one, I suppose. But that was a project that didn't even last ten years. The one I didn't succeed at, and it was a campaign I fought for thirty years, was Graeco-Roman wrestling. You learn that the line between failure and success is as slim as a reflection.

My brother had always been into wrestling. But even when I was six, I could see that what was shown on television was amateur dramatics with sweat. If you couldn't act but you were fat, you could have a career as a wrestler. I didn't get it, and Gary's obsession with sweaty men made me wonder whether he was gay. But sadly, my opinion wasn't shared by billions of people.

But the Olympic sport, Graeco-Roman wrestling, one of the original Olympic sports. People don't get to see it, although the wrestlers are proper athletes in that they took steroids moderately and didn't wear ridiculous costumes. I was convinced it needed serious marketing, and it could really take off. I did decades of meetings, but nothing happened. You never know. When I started it wasn't simply that no one watched women's football. No one even knew it existed.

Does everyone have a mystery? Maybe there's a mystery in many relationships. Their ends. Why do friendships peg out? Sometimes there's something you can point at. Someone behaves badly at a wedding. Someone doesn't turn up at a wedding. A dispute over an egg slicer. Someone, like Dimitri, becomes too dangerous to know. Someone moves to the other side of the world. Why didn't it work out with Vikki? I learned that you have to be paying attention when you're losing, but that you need to pay even more attention when you think you're winning. We're playthings of chance.

฿

My Big Cousin was smarter and tougher than me. And bigger. Not much smarter and tougher than me, but he was. It was frustrating, because there's nothing you can do. Staying up late, plotting, more push-ups, there was no way to catch up with him. All his girlfriends were so beautiful, I could barely talk to them.

I only got the better of him once. A chicken vindaloo challenge. My Big Cousin said he could out-vindaloo me. I reckoned I would lose, but you couldn't chicken out of a challenge.

It was a different era. If you were male and you went to the Indian, you had to have the vindaloo, to show how nails you were. I suppose the vindaloo was the first dish to have real kick ever in the British Isles. It was like McDonalds. The first one opened in Catford, and whatever you think of the burger lords, it was dazzling sophistication compared to what came before. A large step for mankind. In the 70s if your high street had an Indian, a Chinese, and a burger joint, you were living in Paris, on the fucking Left Bank.

The place we went to was called the Curry House. It was the seventies, just to make it clear. If you named your curry joint the Taj Mahal or the Red Fort no one would have known what it was. You might as well have called it the Vatican Laundromat. Or the Inner Space Exploration Society. They were generous with the oil and the portions, really generous. No one wanted to be a fat bastard, but having a big appetite, shovelling it in like an excavator, was a sign of an appetite for life, of all-round dominance.

It meant you did women all night long. You were fireproof. You were dangerous. Beyond control.

"I had a fun visit to Camberwell this afternoon," my Big Cousin said. He also did some work as a debt collector for a reggae record company. He'd trawl around London reminding people with bad memories, coaxing cash out of registers. "Some dippy hippy running a place with a rank amount of Prog Rock. Can you believe he gave me some grief?"

"No," I said, because I found it hard to believe some lentil-eater would say anything to my Big Cousin apart from, "Yes, sir, would you like a Roger Dean poster?" But this is one of the interesting things, a curious, spooky phenomenon, right out of quantum, that people with no fight will pick a fight with people with buckets of fight. When everyone knows that is the situation. At school, a kid in the year below me, smaller than me, soft as potato puree, called me out, for no reason at all. I didn't want to fight, I didn't want to hurt him, but I had no choice. I did him with a chair leg and sent him to hospital.

"He was really cheeky," my Big Cousin continued. "I had to superglue a Tangerine Dream album to his face."

I spluttered into my beer.

"No, wait, wait, that's not the punchline. The punchline is, he goes to me 'I'm calling the police.' And I say, 'I am the police, pal.'"

My Big Cousin was the police. To an extent. He was a Special Constable at a very special police station, Catford nick. Depending on your point of view it was the worst police station in London because many were on the take and they did things like murder. Or it was the best because they could always find evidence, somehow, to convict serious criminals.

"You know how many years I've been waiting to use that line?"

My Big Cousin gave up on the third vindaloo. There wasn't much left on his plate, two mouthfuls of chicken and some scoops of rice.

I had won the showdown. Except it didn't count. I knew I hadn't beaten him in a fair fight. I could see he was ill. Tired. Off-colour. Something. Down in the mouth because he had achieved a major goal.

"That's impressive," he said to me. But it wasn't. I recognized the tone. The tone when an adult praises a kid's drawing. They say the best general never has to fight a battle. I'd go one more. I'd say the top general gets the other side to believe they've won. Magnificently.

I'd lucked out. I was a grain of rice away from puking. Afterwards I didn't go home. I had to walk off my full guts for four hours. Many years later I re-examined the look on my Big Cousin's face and saw clearly how he was preoccupied.

฿

There was the mystery of my Big Cousin's death. It seemed wrong. Died in a fire. Of course, fires kill, usually not from the fire but the smoke. That's what gets you. My Big Cousin was in many ways more like my older brother than my older brother. That's not a bad reflection on Gary. It's like grandparents get the best of childhood with the grandkids – they can skip the more grinding bits. My Big Cousin never had to share a bedroom with me.

To lose it all. You only have to be unlucky once. The bad luck only has to sneak though the defences once. You only have to be a little slow, a little careless. Not looking crossing the road once, and you're squashed.

My Aunt was relentless about locking and bolting up her place whenever she went out even though she really had nothing worth stealing. For nineteen years she locked up her place, then one summer, she went out for ten minutes, and as it was so hot, left one window slightly open. When she got back, she had been burgled. The loot amounted to a small bottle of gin, her best orchid and an egg slicer. But what boiled her spuds was that she hadn't closed the window. If the window had just been smashed, it could have been written off as one of those things.

It could have been that my Big Cousin had a few drinks and was out of it. He wasn't a serious boozer, but we all have boys' nights where things can go too swingingly. Bearing in mind he was a Special Constable at the bentest nick in London, and the crowd he knew, you couldn't help wondering, was it really an accident? The doubt did nag me.

If it happened now, I have the resources and the smarts to hire some experts to do some poking. But I didn't then, and also, I wasn't sufficiently blackened to challenge everyone. One of his police mates said it all checked out, electrical fire. Now I know with certainty you can't trust anyone, especially experts. You want to be sure, or to get as close to a surety you can live with, you have to keep swinging.

I got my Big Cousin's knuckleduster, one of his few possessions that made it through the fire. I've kept it.

₿

We might have been good stress druids, but the firm never had a player in the top hundred. A few who bobbed in the three hundreds briefly, but most of our clients were in the six hundreds. Fodder at the grand slams. We all earned a living.

Some say the top players are self-centred, temperamental. I say that's unfair. They're no longer human. You can't be at that level.

I met him for the first time in the taxi rank at Miami airport. When he was seventeen or so. He was behind me in the queue. A few days before I'd watched him spank the world number 446 in Basel with, and this is the key, with almost no effort. None of the grunting, panting theatricals. He looked as if he was doing the washing-up.

"I'm Cannon," he said as I introduced myself and offered him a ride since we were staying at the same hotel. He didn't have an entourage guarding him, which surprised me. I knew a free ride wouldn't count for much, but you have to start somewhere. A South African, he was the most talented player I'd ever seen at that age. He was far better than anyone we had on the books. It almost seemed wrong to recruit him. He deserved better than us. "Great win in Basel," I went. That got zero response, but then if you cared about anything anyone said, you wouldn't be spanking number 446. Delicately, I quizzed him about who looked after him.

When we were checking in at the hotel, he swore as he got a message inviting him to some swanky soiree. "I haven't got anything but tennis gear."

When you travel a lot, packing becomes an art. You learn to have a few essentials with you, even though it adds weight. A tie. A white shirt. A smart jacket. One item of warm clothing, no matter how hot your destination. In Miami, one night, I ended up sleeping in every item of clothing I had, because there was a cold front, and my hotel room had no heating, because you don't need that in Miami.

As he was roughly my size, I offered Cannon the shirt, the tie and the jacket. In the taxi he had been as chatty as a block of granite, so I coached him on one or two tennis jokes in case he was called on to say a few words. Casually, I handed him my card, suggesting if he were ever in London, I'd buy him a drink. Gratitude was obviously out of the question, but he did notice me for the first time, that I wasn't some massive insect buzzing around. Maybe, one day, we can druid your stress, Cannon, I thought. I studied the large, ugly skull and crossbones earring in his left ear. Doubt the sponsors will go for that. Unless someone needs a bad boy. Sometimes they do.

Did I get my clothes back? Of course not. To be fair, it's

possible Cannon entrusted them to someone at the hotel who then couldn't be arsed. Rosamund allowed me to claim the loss as expenses, though noted: "We're supposed to take the shirt off our clients' backs, not the other way round. Did you not get the memo?" Still, I thought, this is an investment. Me and Cannon then passed a couple of times in corridors. I couldn't raise the missing clothes, but I gave Cannon friendly nods, got something back, but it might have been reflex. I get nodders, I smile and nod back. Why not?

Cannon was rising. About a year after I sacrificed my jacket, I saw that he was encroaching. In the charts at number 199. If nothing else I felt pleased about my judgement. There's something bracing about being right, even if it doesn't help you much. I popped out for lunch and I returned with my kebab, with extra chilli to power me through the afternoon. I always went for the extra chilli.

Gina had been with me, after her return from her trip to Ibiza, for a couple of weeks. I'd always had a fear that if I left the office at lunchtime for a bite, that would be when the important call would come, while I was out scoffing something. The Big Moment would breeze past. If nothing else, Gina planted in the office meant I was covered if Destiny took a peek.

When I returned to the office munching on my kebab, Carjack Carlo was talking to Gina. "I'd never had a gun waved in my face."

Carlo was one of our accountants and he was talking about the best day of his life. He was telling Gina the story of how he had been driving past Brixton prison one afternoon when a prisoner had escaped and waved a pistol at Carlo to steal his car. It was a true story and a great anecdote, but it was the only one Carlo had. He told it a lot, at any opportunity. Most of us in the office could repeat it word for word.

I worked with him for years, but I can't remember anything

else he said. I was down on him at the time for banging on about it, but I realized years later that it wasn't his fault he was event-poor. Just as it wasn't Dimitri's fault he was constantly dicing with death, Carlo wasn't to blame for that one minute being the only marketable thing he had to say. At least he had that one cracker. And it makes you realize that there must be people who get to the finish line without even the one stonking yarn to brandish. The Wheel distributes.

Gina saw me and got up to go and get her lunch.

"It's unbelievable,' she said as I took my last bite of kebab and tossed the wrapping into a bin on the other side of the office. My aim was true.

"What?"

"People think they can just walk in here and get us to represent them. Someone came in asking for you while you were out. Said he was a tennis player, but he didn't even have a racket.'

"What was his name?'

"Can't remember. He was a bit mumbly. Conan. Canine? He had a funny accent."

"South African?"

"More Australian. But I explained him we only work with top players and he should come back when he had won something. And a racket. Who does he think he is?"

"When did he leave?'

"About twenty minutes ago."

"He didn't have a big earring, did he? A skull and crossbones?'

"He did. Someone you know then? Honestly, who does he think he is, swanning in here?"

He thinks he's the world 199. This week. You arrive unprepared. You learn too late. This was another one of the proudest moments of my life. I surprised myself. With my self-control. With my perspective. Maybe this was the moment I became what you might call an adult. A man. A young man, with a lot to learn, but a man. I didn't scream. I didn't kick a table or punch a wall. I was a little dizzy, so I leaned on my desk.

Was it my fault that the world number 199 had been shown the door? That the firm's long battle for getting someone in the top two hundred had slipped away? No, it wasn't. And really that was our daily routine, not getting the big boys and girls. I wasn't doing anything the others weren't.

It was Gina's fault. How hard would it have been to say, well, "Dan'll be back soon if you'd like to wait."

But her fault could be seen as my fault. Had I given her clear instructions on how to deal with walk-ins? No, I hadn't because we'd never had a player walk in before, and you'd hope a fellow human being would have some sense.

I looked around to see if there were grinning faces. To see if the gloaters were grinning. To see if my disaster had been passed around the office like a box of chocs. No. Tedium ruled. I could see the boss in his office, picking his nose.

If something terrible has happened, but no one knows about it, then basically it hasn't happened. No one else in the office knew Cannon by sight. Carlo did numbers, not players. Nearly everyone else had been out for lunch. The era of delivery hadn't arrived. No one was going to ask me if Cannon had signed. I wasn't going to be fired over this loss, but I could end up as the office laughing stock. One of the classic timeless anecdotes of the office.

"Yeah," I said. "I know him. He's some nutter that wanders into offices trying it on. Rather sad. I'm glad I wasn't here. Well done. Nicely handled." It was my finest hour. Cool. Cutting myself surgically out of the tangle. Misdirection. Nothing to see here, a nutter dispatched. I don't know how I did it.

I did consider a rescue mission, but if you've taken the trouble to locate an office and go there and be told to bugger off? No one with a small ego or forgiving nature can survive at that level.

I left the office early, went to Greenwich Park, which was

almost empty, and screamed for half an hour. I saw some policemen approaching as I left the park. My guts were in a mess for a week from the swallowed rage, I woke up in the early hours of the morning, spud-boiling. It did occur to me that this was some careful punishment being meted out to me for failing to get David Bowie's autograph.

And Gina had to go. She was bad news. You can see individuals like that at a distance. You can see they're trouble. They're not having a bad day, they're not unlucky. They're trouble. You can be walking on a huge, wide pavement. And you'll see them yards off, and you know whether you go to the right or the left, slow down or speed up, they will get in your way. They're the passengers in the check-in queue in front of you, who are unable check in for a variety of bizarre reasons. Gina had to go. And she did, but not before one other major play.

Cannon? He had some tough matches, five set thrillers he lost by a handful of points against top ten monsters. He slipped into the mid three hundreds. But he'd been signed by the apex predators. I wasn't the only one that had my eye on him.

Cannon's inevitable rise stopped rising. He went for a stroll in The Black Forest. A quiet lane. A car ploughed into him, smashed his hips, femurs. I felt sorry for him, but to be honest, it made me feel a little better about Gina bundling him out of the office. Cannon got to walk again and play tennis again, but not on the circuit.

I had seen him play shots that didn't seem real. They defied physics. How do you do that? It was like cheating. It was like watching a special effect in a film. If you've been gifted that, if you've played a forehand that only God could have managed, and the knowers are there to applaud it, is it reasonable to expect more? When have you've had a good deal? Got what you deserved? A serving of fairness?

If you want to play tennis and if only for two minutes you do it better than anyone else on the planet, isn't that enough? Even if the crowds don't notice?

฿

Really, it's surprising more people don't kill each other. Or maybe they do, but no one notices.

She was queuing up for a gig, near Clapham Junction, the first time I met Vikki. She was with a friend, Susan, who I vaguely knew. We were introduced. A nod. No more. No thunderclap. At that age you always hope that when you're introduced to an attractive woman you'll unleash some curiosity. Vikki carried on staring at the pavement, bored by queuing.

I was on my way to see Battersea Bill. My Big Cousin had introduced me. The big London exodus to Brighton had only just started. Prospective rock stars, ailing rock stars, graphic designers, poets, they had figured out they didn't need to pay London rent. Once a month or so I'd take a package of coke down to Brighton, hand it over to the organist at the big church on the seafront, who'd then spread it around. This was the early eighties, when coke was a niche market. Mostly kids from the posho schools and singers who wanted to be David Bowie. It wasn't like it is now, when you can order it with your pint and crisps at your local. With all the chic of a sausage roll.

Bill was raided quite often. It took the police many years to work out his stash was in the flat above his, occupied by a librarian who'd been in Auschwitz. Bill would bang on the ceiling with a broom, and goods would be lowered in a basket at the back window. I'd got on well with Bill until that evening. Roar Meat, who'd been a punk drummer and whose job seemed to be hanging out at Bill's, and putting on weight to add to his already astonishing weight, let me in.

Bill liked to talk. He talked a lot about industrial lubricants.

Strange oils. He used to sell them and I got the impression he missed that job. Collecting a package could take hours.

But that evening Bill didn't say hello. He didn't say a word. He gave me a furious glare. His jaw was moving as if he were chewing something unchewable. Like the proverbial bulldog with a wasp in its mouth. Roar produced a cutlass. It wasn't some crappy prop from a panto. It was a sharp, proper, gleaming cutlass. As used by pirates. Professionals. For killing people. Where do you get one of those?

"You're fucking dead,' Bill screamed.

"What did you do with that last delivery?" Roar roared.

"Nothing," I was squeaking like a large mouse.

"The poof organist says you didn't deliver. We want our goods. We'll chop you up." Roar cut the air with gusto. And slashed my coat. It was my best coat. I'd almost wept when I'd bought it, it was so expensive.

"I . . . I gave him the package." I had given him the package. Those words took a lot of effort. It was like mountaineering. To say I was scared was a real understatement. I was near fainting.

Bill and Roar started laughing. "Your face," Bill said. They laughed so hard Bill was crying. Roar slumped to the floor, hooting. Seeing them rolling around, I eventually figured out this was a joke. I'm glad they laughed for a very long time because it gave me a chance to pull myself together.

It was at this moment I decided to stop being a mule. Obviously, I didn't tell them that, because I didn't want it to look like I'd lost my bottle. I had my job at the firm, and while the extra money from Bill was very welcome, I had definitely lost my bottle. They gave me a drink and they thought we had a chat, but my contribution was nodding as Bill got back onto his theme of how the public at large didn't appreciate the sophistication and range of industrial lubricants. Their importance. Probably they felt a little bad about the prank, and they weren't the type to feel bad.

It might have been crime, but, like any employer, they knew it was hard to find employees who would turn up punctually and do some of what they're asked to do.

Later that night I got on the last train to Brighton to deliver my last package. As I worked my way down the carriage, I saw Vikki sitting on her own. I don't think I would have recognized her, but she had been wearing a scarlet jacket with a high collar. It was the sort of thing the queen of a small country would wear and was the loudest item in her wardrobe. Out of courtesy, and because I didn't have a paper to read (different era) I sat down, relieved I could remember her name.

I was a young man, I knew that you should talk to women, because they tended to know other women. And you never knew. I can't believe what I did in those days. I reintroduced myself as Dan because I was sure she wouldn't remember.

"How was the gig?" I asked. She had fantastic tennis-ball firm breasts.

"Okay," she said. "They only had one good song. 'Let's do it sideways'."

That's creativity. How many songs are there about doing it? Let's do it, baby. Let's do it right now. Let's do it in the road. Why aren't we doing it? You just have to give it a twist, don't you? Freshen it up. Do it sideways. I hadn't heard that before.

Suddenly Vikki changed from pavement-starer. Probably because she didn't have anything to read and it's a long hour in the dark to Brighton, she fancied company. Her face changed. "So, Dan, tell me about yourself."

And she gave me the full frontal. I was being auditioned. I was being challenged. Let's see what you've got, big boy. I also saw something I'd never seen in a woman's face, certainly not at that point, a vast hinterland. It's unfortunate, but you rarely find someone interesting who's had a smooth life. And she had this great nose. Really sharp, like a bird of prey. A falcon. Hawk. Haughty, fearless.

She asked me about my slashed coat. "Caught on some bushes." She obviously didn't believe me. Rightly so. One thing I've never done with women is wax it up. I'm a fighter pilot. I'm a millionaire, but my Rolls Royce is being resprayed. I've always been straight, but I didn't think the truth in this instance was worth going into.

We went through the basics. I was hoping Vikki might ask for a ticket to Wimbledon when I told her what I did, but she didn't. She had just finished a physics degree and was doing research into quantum mechanics.

"What's quantum?' I asked. What extraordinary tits.

"It's hard to explain," she said. She looked around in an over-the-top conspiratorial way. There was no one in earshot. "I'll let you into a secret," she whispered. "No one can explain it." She was clearly not at all concerned with explaining it to bloke with boner on last train to Brighton. I made a note next time I passed a bookshop to pop in and see if they had a title I could flick through like "Enough quantum to get laid' etc.

"Inanity," Vikki said. "There's a whole lot of nothing out there, in the universe. Everything is nothing. The nothing is thicker in some places than others."

"The nothing is thicker?"

"The harder you look, the more nothing there is. When you hug someone, you're hugging nothing."

"Hugging nothing . . . because there's nothing else to do?"

"That would be a good lyric."

She spoke about fission and fusion. I didn't have a clue about what she was saying. I like to think I managed to keep that to myself. Poker Face. Everyone says I have one. Hardly anyone can tell when I'm joking or serious. Perhaps I should have played poker. Vikki talked about nuclear explosions like I would talk about topspin forehands.

"You need to enrich the uranium," she said. "It's not that difficult. You need a nuclear reactor."

"Your university had a reactor?'

"An itsy-bitsy one."

"Are you telling me you did a course at university on how to make a nuclear bomb?'

"They didn't call it that."

There are all sorts of things you just don't know about. Worlds sprawled around the world. Maybe it's better that you don't. The idea that students, those twats who spent years doing pub crawls dressed up as nuns and stealing traffic cones, had access to a nuclear reactor freaked me.

Beauty, and its spin-offs, is a word that means nothing. Beauty used so often, by so many mouths, in so many ways, it's been flogged to death. Rubbed away into invisibility. At most a grunt of approval. We need to invent a new word. Let's have a competition.

I didn't fully sense it at the time; there was something in Vikki I hadn't seen before. Or at least you could argue I thought there was something there. I think there was.

I didn't know it but that night was going to be the beginning of a long era of having the object of my desires, hundreds, thousands of miles away. A long period of long-distance love, where my other half tended to be where I wasn't. The Wheel. The Wheel.

Vikki playfully kept her boyfriend's existence hidden until we were pulling into Brighton. It was a cold, dark night. I had told her I was visiting a friend. But I had been planning the old, I'm not sure whether I have a place to stay routine. Why not? But I didn't mind she wasn't single. I was patient. I could wait my turn. I had a host of phone numbers of women I was waiting for. I was waiting for their relationships to crash and burn. Plan ahead.

But I was still considering the let-me escort-you-home routine, because it at least establishes you as chivalrous, and I know that sometimes even a fifteen-minute walk and fresh air can bring about a dramatic change of heart. And you know exactly where they live. Groundwork. Anyone in sports, business, can tell you the importance of good prep.

But then an old lady started going off. Had a turn and slumped on the platform. I don't know what she was doing on the last train to Brighton. Vikki stayed to dear-dear her while the ambulance arrived. I'd had a long day being threatened with cutlasses etc. I slipped Vikki my card and I realized I wasn't getting her number back.

Never mind. I had to deliver coke to an organist who always grumbled about pianists, guitarists, violinists, essentially any musician who didn't play the organ, making money. He would make the same joke about how a successful organist was an organist who had a wife with two jobs. He eventually did a bit of time for noncing. There's something reassuring about stereotypes. All's in order. He always offered me place to sleep.

As I walked down to the seaside, it dawned on me the conversation I'd had with Vikki was like something I'd never had. I was twenty-two, but I felt more adult afterwards. When you play someone much better, it's painfully humiliating. Really painful. But when you play someone better, you often up your game, even if you lose. Vikki had coached me in some way. Freshened me up. Straightened me up. I'd had the cutlass wiped from memory.

I stayed the night at the pub run by the Hells Angels. Bill had put me in touch with them in the hope that they'd get on the coke train. When I was young, you'd see them riding around, but by this point they were fat and had discovered that a car will keep you dry and warm in the rain, and you can pack more gear into them. They'd ride out once in a while at the weekends, like going to church, because they had to.

They were always friendly to me and I got them tickets to Wimbledon. But coke didn't interest them (apart from the freebies Bill sent). They owned clubs and pubs, controlled the speed and weed and didn't see the need for coke. "Shitty dago speed," was one observation. Because they had no need for coke. They were sitting pretty. The bankers who sniffed at crypto at first and told it to move along reminded me of those tubby bikers.

There was a huge comic shop in Lewisham. Huge. I spent most of my pocket money there as a kid. It's embarrassing to admit, but some of the best moments of my life were reading comics. I used to dream about the shop a lot. I've never believed in the interpretation of dreams. My dreams never needed a commentary. If you're dreaming about a naked German Game Show Hostess, no explanation required. In my dreams I'd be walking into the comic shop, excited, again and again, long after it had closed down. Decades after. It represented escape. Hope. Comics were better. They were what life should be like. It was escape into a better world. A sort of heaven.

I don't have that dream anymore.

₿

The week after, I was replaying my chat with Vikki, examining my technique. Could I have played it better and got a hook in? Could I have got her number? It was certain she wouldn't call me. I was annoyed with myself, but it was, on reflection, a no-win scenario. Hey ho. I'd done my best.

Does everyone get a totally improbable event? I'd already had one, with Bowie, but I got another. I was getting off the tube at South Kensington, and as the doors opened, Vikki was right in front of me. Not at the far end of the platform, not a few feet away down the platform, but right, directly in front of me. Like a tourist, or volunteer moron, blocking my exit. As if it had been arranged.

"Hello," I said, getting off. Vikki smiled in amusement. It was so improbable, so surprising, getting exactly what I wanted, on a plate, that I nearly blew it. I actually took one or two steps away. I actually walked away. It was only at the last second that I jumped back on the train to suggest a coffee. It was all so improbable. I suspect she wanted to say no, but had to say yes. We got off at Gloucester Road.

Again, you arrive unprepared. The immediate unprepares you. I was sitting there listening to more nuclear stories, plotting how do I sink another hook? There were two delicate mentions of her boyfriend, some piano technician, whatever that was, just to make things clear. I sat there thinking I'm enjoying talking with you more than shagging the woman I had been invited to entertain in South Kensington, who was doubtless wondering where the hell I was. I'm enjoying the chat a lot more.

I hoped people noticed me with her. Look it's me, having coffee with this beautiful, intelligent woman, who might blow up the planet. In the way I had hoped people would notice me with the girl with biggest tits when I was sixteen. It was like sitting with the bad boys at the back of class. Felt great. I could have sat there with her until two in the morning. I just didn't want it to end. I gave her my card again, belt and braces. I offered her coffee if she were in town again, and of course, Wimbledon tickets (although I knew we had run out of our allocation). But it looked like that was that.

There was a bookshop, as I trudged my way back to South Ken to do my duty. I guess it was the first time I'd gone into a bookshop, and I got angry because they had nothing on the lines of "Nuclear secrets for shaggers". My performance in South Ken was floppy. Whatever my faults, I don't like to disappoint. I've always been grateful to employers (maybe not Bill) and grateful to women who've admitted me to their beds. Because you're not entitled to anything.

A month later, as I was leaving the office. I got a phone call.

"It's Vikki. Vikki from Brighton." I liked that. Not sure I'd place her. My service. Fifteen-love. "Listen, Dan, I was going to a piano recital tonight with a friend, but she can't make it. Would you like to come?" Would I like to go to a piano recital? Of course not. No, absolutely fucking not. Would I like to go to a piano recital with you? Well, well.

Her friend couldn't make it because her dog had been puking up violently. I could have lived without that detail. Our first date of sorts, courtesy of a spewing Spaniel. Vikki did mention the boyfriend again, delicate signposting. To be clear. But for some reason she didn't want to go to the recital alone. We all have our peculiarities. I could have lived without the piano recital.

I sat there watching some Oriental woman tapping a piano and I looked around at the audience. Why are we here? Is this some weird cult? I'd offered to pay for my ticket, super chivalrous, and I spent most of the evening bitterly regretting that. What a con. But we had a footing now. There was glue now. We had one drink before she had to rush off for the Brighton train.

'What's the story with the scar, Dan?"

"You may not know this, but water is dangerous."

The piano business bothered me. I just couldn't understand it. I bought a CD of Haydn's sonatas. An impulse buy, because it was on sale. With a massive discount, otherwise I would have passed. I played it and I still didn't get it. I almost threw it out I was so outraged by the waste of money.

It was a different era. This is when CDs were expensive, were worshipped like holy relics. Alien tech. But doing my laundry one day, listening for the sixth or seventh go, something clicked. No, it was rather some door opened and I got inside. Those sonatas became my fleeing the world refuge, my foxhole, when I needed to lie down and let events pass above me.

It did take me many, many years to understand why. Because there's nothing human there. No sapiens leaving their stains. A purity cleansed of humanity. No one squawking about the condition of their ego, their games. Their wins. Their losses. A lot of music is too peopley. A Haydn sonata, it's a trip somewhere else. Like a primeval forest. The far side of Jupiter. Somewhere clean, shiny, serene. No oozy emotion. All that.

"Music, music, that's nothing but stored emotion." That was Vikki's line. That's certainly true of some music. Maybe she's right after all, and the emotion I thought I was dodging in Haydn was in fact the emotion of freedom from humanity. From myself?

฿

I had to attack. When I was thirteen, I got to know a girl. We kissed, because that was what you were supposed to do. It was like stepping into a fire. We found ourselves at the head of a queue of millions of years of lust. Evolution gave us a mighty shove. We were both taken aback by what we felt. Dazed as if we had had an accident. We had discovered something new. Big. Very big.

With Vikki, it was again landing on a new continent. I couldn't stop thinking about her. What was annoying, was I couldn't figure out why. Vikki wasn't the only attractive, intelligent woman in the country. But Vikki was something new. A step up. Why couldn't there be a fascinating woman without a boyfriend down the road? Why did she have to be in Brighton?

No good sitting around. I had to attack. I had to take it to Brighton. She had made the mistake of giving me her address. I bought and studied the street map of Brighton, like a general. How could I organize some accidental meeting? Not too stalkery. Honestly, I'm not here to remove your clothing, I was just passing by.

Tennis. There's always tennis. Hardly anyone outside of the game appreciates how many tournaments and events there are around the country. Of course, there was a tennis tournament in Brighton. But not for a while.

Then there was the university where Vikki was doing her stuff.

I had no idea when she was likely to be there, which building she worked in. That was high risk and while I had a convincing excuse for hanging round tennis courts, a university would be the last place I'd be sightseeing.

Then there was Jabs. Jabs. We had some bigmouth come to the firm on a high salary claiming he could bring us boxers. Whatever dark stuff takes place in tennis, we were nothing, we were innocent toddlers compared to boxing, which really should just be called organized crime, as they regularly solved problems by killing nuisances. And they were very organized. So, we got nowhere. Bigmouth left. Our handful of boxers who hadn't know better, left. Except for Jabs.

As his nickname suggests he wasn't a great boxer. He was a very heavy heavyweight. He didn't duck. He didn't dive. He couldn't box at all, apart from the jab. Jabs was also a little misleading, in that the plural might make you think he had more than one jab, left and right. No, he only had the right jab. And it wasn't a lightning jab. That was the entire bag of tools.

What had got him a minor career was that he was impossible to knock out. If there's such a thing as a glass jaw, he had a titanium jaw. And a titanium gut. And to be fair if he couldn't box, he had learned one lesson. Keep your guard up. And if you do that, you don't get the hits to the head too often. I've read stories about mafia bosses who were so fat, they were shot six times at close range but just went home for supper because the fat acted as bullet-proofing. There was something like that going on with Jabs. You could pound away at his midriff and nothing much would happen.

I only saw him fight once, against a ripped, tanned, fast guy, who jived around and pummelled him with classy combos, like Jabs was a punchbag. It was so one-sided, there was booing a minute in. Round after round. The guy next to me said it was the most embarrassing fight he'd ever seen. One outraged spectator actually climbed into the ring to show Jabs a few moves. But, by the end you could see Speedy had overdone it and was exhausted. And guess what? Probably after seeing so many right jabs, he was waiting for a left, and Jabs caught him with the right. Knocked out.

His file landed on my desk. Rosamund felt sorry for him. He was like a lost six-year-old. Rosamund was totally unsuited to management in many ways. But not all.

"Dan, I'm handing Jabs over to you," she announced.

"Yes, but . . ."

"I know what you're going to say."

"No, seriously, I . . ."

"Dan, you're the only person in this firm who can do something for him. You're the trickster. The lord of the artful. I do know all about your little dodges. Don't think I don't. I'm asking you for this favour, because you're the best I have. Only you can pull this off."

She'd got me. Jabs was from Bermondsey but had moved to Brighton. His trainer wanted to get rid of him, I suspect, and had given him some guff about how the oxygen was more oxygeny on the coast and he'd train better, and how seagull eggs were the best and good luck. I opened the file that I had not opened up, despite Rosamund's urgings. I had a number for Jabs, but no address. I gave him a call. Wherever he was in Brighton, he could be moved, deployed like a platoon. He had legs, unlike the tennis courts or the university.

"Jabs. Mate. How are you? Listen we don't have an address for you on file, yeah. Don't worry. Don't worry, that's exactly what I'm going to do. I'll be coming down. Coming down soon. No, you really don't have to come up to London. No, I'll come down to Brighton. We aim to please. Honestly, I can come down to Brighton. It's no trouble. No trouble at all. Stress? Yeah, that's our job to druid that. Take care of stress. We are the stress druids. I need some of that top notch oxygen too. How are you? What, a seagull? Yeah, seagulls, they are vicious, aren't they? Super-rats. Absolute super-rats."

Bingo. He lived a couple of streets from Vikki. Mind you, Brighton. Nothing's more than a couple of streets away from anything. I wondered whether I should just announce in advance I was in town and raise the odds of actually meeting Vikki. As opposed to gambling that somehow our paths would cross. But it would be so good to be there, unannounced. Just doing business. And I could always go back again. Rosamund had told me to go out of my way for Jabs.

So, I sat in a café with Jabs. I had chosen the café carefully, likely to be on the route Vikki would take if she were going to town or the university. I had a good seat looking out onto the street. I'd only been listening to Jabs complaining about seagulls savaging him for five minutes or so, when Vikki walked past.

I shot out of my seat and ran out onto the street and yelled after her. I got a big smile. Natural. She was pleased to see me. A result.

"What are you doing here?" she asked.

"Having a meeting with a client," I said. I was uncertain whether it would be a good idea to get Vikki and Jabs together. No, I was going to play it cool. Again, I'd got what I wanted. Okay, brilliant engineering, but it had been a long shot. If I invited her in or asked for a drink, it might look engineered I thought, because it was. I suddenly felt bad about the engineering, was worried that I looked desperate to see her, because I was so desperate to see her.

Then Stag pulled up. Noisily. I'd never seen one of the Brighton Hells Angels on a bike. But here was Stag, on a bike, in full regalia, accompanied by his paunch. I'd definitely chosen the café where the action was. I'd just have to front it out.

"Stag, this is my friend Vikki." Something I never thought I'd say.

"We all know Vikki," said Stag. Brighton, I hate you. "So, Dan the Pusherman, how's the cocaine trade?"

Then, Jabs, who must have been feeling lonely, came out, barely fitting through the café door and stood behind me. Like something lumbering out of Frankenstein's lab.

"Now that's what I call a bodyguard," said Stag. "Business is good, huh?"

Vikki and Stag exchanged some gossip. Vikki knew Stag's girlfriend. Jabs asked for advice about how to steal seagull eggs. I felt enormous sympathy for God, if he existed. Maybe he had started out with a plan . . .

"You should have warned me you were coming," said Vikki as we parted. "I'm off to the beach for some rays. Did you know we have a nudist beach? You don't have to worry about any white bits."

Later on, I never asked her whether she was winding me up or not. Because she did go there from time to time.

"She's your fan, do you know that? You've got a welcome there," Jabs stated. About the only thing he said that didn't involve seagulls. Did he have some weird clairvoyance that compensated him for being a thick six-year-old? Should he be telling fortunes on Brighton Pier? I hoped so, because boxing wasn't going to get him anywhere. A boxer who couldn't box, managed by a firm that didn't care about boxing and knew nothing about it. It was so improbable an arrangement, as improbable as Bitcoin, it should have been a success, but it wasn't.

His remark did make me feel better. Reassurance works. A bit. For a while. Like aspirin. I know because I've done it with clients. Insincerely.

I had a restless night. How to regroup? Could I just claim that Stag was pulling her leg? How well did she know Stag? Could I laugh off the coke as a bit of loveable roguery? A lark? She didn't look at all perplexed by my being in league with internationally known criminal organisations? Was there a lot more to discover about Vikki? Did she want a wrap?

฿

It continued to bother me that I couldn't get Vikki out of my mind. At a party, I met a tall brunette. She had fantastic legs. I can't say I'm a legs man or a breast man, because I've always gone for every part of the body.

"I'm so lucky," she said. "I work for David Bowie's management company. It's like being paid to have a good time. He's such a great guy. So much fun to be around."

"I met him once," I said.

"Oh, where?"

"He rang my doorbell. He needed to use the phone."

"Oh, sod off," she laughed. She shook with laughter. I think it was the most successful line I've ever said to a woman. I was in good shape in those years, but this was the only time in my life when I succeeded in pulling in a matter of hours. It was made abundantly clear. "It's a bit noisy and stuffy here, isn't it, we could go back to my place for a drink?" It wasn't noisy or stuffy. She had astonishing legs and I'm sure she was one of those women who put a lot of effort and cash into lingerie. I was wondering where Vikki was. What she was doing? What I could do?

"I'd love to," I said. "But sorry, I have to catch a flight to Johannesburg in about four hours. Still have to pack." I still think about her legs. It should have been a novel thrill, like fucking a lighthouse. But I knew I couldn't deliver. It would have been churlish. It would have been more like throwing my clothes into the washing machine half-asleep on a Sunday morning.

฿

Dimitri phoned me.

"You have boxers, don't you?'

"We have one. He's not winning anything."

"Is he available for something extra-curricular?"

"How extra-curricular?"

"Would he want to earn a few extra quid?"

"He'd probably mow your lawn for beans on toast."

Dimitri had problems with an insurance company. They were based in Gibraltar. They hadn't paid out on his roofing claim. Flat out refused, without even doing the pretending to consider it bit. They were an insurance company, so obviously they weren't going to pay out. And an insurance company based in Gibraltar? Why Dimitri had used them, it was like calling yourself Rip-Off and Sons. Plus being based in Gibraltar, they enjoyed some security from irate, shouty Brits. Insulation.

"I want them done. Nothing too serious," said Dimitri. "Some mashing up. Broken nose. Fractured rib. Can you kneecap someone without a gun?"

"I wouldn't complicate it. I sure he could do a general pasting that'd make you proud."

"I'd really appreciate it if you could sort this out."

As soon as Dimitri phoned, I had been waiting to bring in Gina. Gina was messing up everything she touched. Sending tickets and money to the wrong people. She'd wrecked the photocopier. I spent more time on damage control than anything else. Rosamund, and everyone else, had noticed that she should be avoided at all costs. However, the boss was ridiculously pally with her mother, so I couldn't fire her.

The solution was simple, if hard to achieve. Get her a better paid job somewhere else, so she'd leave, and leave happy. Dimitri, I have this talented assistant. She'll go far, but she's not getting the education she needs here. She needs to be at a bigger company. I've sort of already promised her a step up, if you know what I mean. She's paid in advance. Can you help me out?

Maybe not the most convincing cover story, but what else? I was leaving it till last, timing it, but then, "Dan, I hate to take advantage of your good nature once more, but I'm real need of an assistant. I just had to fire one who killed our photocopier and sent contracts to the wrong people. I need someone experienced. Battle-hardened. Firing on all cylinders. Anyone steely at your place?"

"No one comes to mind," I said in a thinking-it-over voice. Hold back. Hold back. Let him brew for a bit.

"Do you have an assistant, Dan?'

"Of course."

"Look, I'm frantic, I need someone switched on. Who knows the ropes. I haven't got time to mentor. You know I can make it worth your while. No nonsense. I'm talking about a major bung. Cash in hand."

I gave a sigh.

"Come on, Dan. I got you in. Took you off the street."

"Okay. Okay. But I don't want a bung. I need a favour. I want you to throw one of your come and have a free drink parties, in Brighton."

"I don't know what skulduggery you're up to, but no problem. We do a couple every year. I'd sooner go to Brighton than Doncaster or Penzance, where you have to talk to people with webbed feet. Done deal. Next party's due in . . . four, five months. We'd been thinking of Amsterdam."

"Here's the favour part. I'd like the party, more in say, in two weeks' time."

"That's mad."

"I'll even help set it up. Long as you pay the costs. Gina will be in touch. Sorry, she won't come cheap either."

You think you're on top. You're not. The Wheel. The Wheel.

฿

Anyone who's managed anyone knows there is no such thing as sufficient instructions. Jabs was willing to fly out to sunny Gibraltar to some duffing.

"How are you, Dan?" he asked. A question I was rarely asked by my clients.

"I'm feeling good. Feeling on top."

"No, you're not. Not yet," he said. I don't know why he said that. He knew almost nothing about me. I explained the project to him and he agreed.

Jabs found the insurance office. It was run by three guys. Two of them were there. Jabs actually had boxing gloves on because he didn't want to injure his hands. What a pro. I saw some pictures afterwards. One guy's head looked like a red cabbage. So, Jabs had done the hard part. Found the office. In a slightly foreign country. Mashed them up.

Any professional criminal, particularly one not in prison, will tell you the really important part of any crime is getting away with it. Spain is a ten-minute walk from anywhere in Gibraltar. Gibraltar has an airport. Instead of immediately walking away or walking to the airport, Jabs sat down for a large portion of paella. When you're twice the size of the average citizen in Gibraltar, you're not hard to find.

I felt guilty about Jabs being arrested. He was six years old. I should have added a farewell sentence to him like: "Leave straight away."

As always, I had gone to my Big Cousin.

"Up the game, you tosspot," he said.

"How?"

"You're an insurance company. You're used to having a laugh with single mothers and the terminally ill, the incapable, the feeble. Now, suddenly, some heavyweight from London flies in, bangs your head on your desk until there's no more desk left. What are you thinking?"

"Ow?"

"Are you thinking, that drip from the sports management company is upset about a few quid for a roofing claim, and, because of that, has spunked twenty times that amount shipping the man-mountain over to Gibraltar?"

It was like a difficult maths homework. "Probably not. No." I could see from my Big Cousin's face no was the correct answer.

"What you're thinking is, since you spend your whole day committing crime, you've done something worse, you've fucked up. You've shafted someone you shouldn't have shafted. You've shafted off-limits. Your shafting has gone in the wrong hole. Not a pensioner. Some unemployed organist. Someone very, very heavy."

I nodded. I couldn't see any solution.

"Okay, what do you do now?" My Big Cousin glared at me like my maths teacher.

"I don't know."

"And you're supposed to be the smart one in the family. You up the game. They're going to be shitting themselves, going through their files, looking to see who's behind Jabs, especially the one who got away without having his face redesigned."

"How do I up the game?"

"You write to them."

"I write to them?"

"You write to them, tosspot, and politely ask them, pretty please to drop the charges against your boy. Do it with one of those cards that has flowers on the front. Maybe a bunny rabbit."

Of course, my Big Cousin didn't mean that. He was talking about the tried and trusted method of threatening someone. It was a different era. For only the cost of postage, and a few minutes scribbling, I could send a letter to Gibraltar, suggesting they drop the charges against Jabs, using that classic phrase 'if you know what's good for you'. As I posted the letter, I did wonder does anyone really know what's good for them? That really does seem to be the problem. No one has a clue what's good for them.

It worked. Or at least the charges against Jabs were dropped. He married one of the secretaries at the police station and stayed in Gibraltar. He sent me a postcard, with just the one line. "You're unlucky if you've never been unlucky." I felt I had honoured the firm's obligations.

฿

The do in Brighton was okay. Dimitri's firm held these jamborees to remind everyone that they existed. Buying people a drink, it may not do you any good, but it rarely does any harm. Ours is a social business. Dimitri kept on studying me, trying to figure out my angle, the motive behind my demand. His boss was a few months away from his unfortunate encounter with a golf ball. The company several from its extinction. We hadn't attached Disaster to Dimitri's name just yet.

I had my say on the guest list. Stag and some of his mates worked the canapes hard and had a long discussion with Dimitri about ancient British motorcycles. I gave Vikki a plus one to see what would happen. Would she bring the boyfriend? I wanted to size up the competition.

She turned up with a friend, Evie, who kept expressing astonishment at how fascinating my job was. I suspected Vikki had brought her unattached friend along to feed her to me, to get rid of me. Some other time maybe, but not now. I was organizing international violence like the British Army and putting on spectaculars just to talk to Vikki. I couldn't help thinking things were more complicated than they needed to be. There had to be a more simple, easy way.

"How's the piano-tuner?" I asked. "He's fine," she said in a tone which suggested all was not well. I didn't like the idea of her being unhappy, but I suppose we had to get through it.

Gina's contract had a notice period of two months. I thought she'd be straight out the door the minute Dimitri offered her the better deal. But she insisted on serving it out. "I can't let the firm down," she said. I suspected sarcasm at first, but no. For some inexplicable reason, she insisted on staying, though everyone, from the boss and Rosamund down, insisted, more than once, it would be no problem if she went off to richer pastures.

I was plotting another connection, another camouflaged date (I've just been given these tickets to a piano recital. Can you help me out?), when I got a call from Vikki.

"I might come up to London this weekend. I need a change of scene. Are you around?" We agreed she'd give me a call on the Friday.

"If you don't hear from me, forget it," she said. "It means I'm not coming."

I had that dangerous winning sensation. I felt the piano-tuner was hitting false notes. I sat in the office until late. No call. I was disappointed, but things happen, we all change our minds etc. I tried her number but no reply. I could take a blow or two. I wasn't going to give up.

Monday morning, as I was dealing with a whining footballer, Gina said. "I almost forgot. A Vikki called you Friday. Said she was coming up to London. Does that make sense?" It was the only time I seriously considered hitting a woman. I really thought about it. In fact, I still do. But I did go berserk. My Poker Face broke badly.

It was a while before I found out Vikki had come to London. She had gone to a party that weekend. Had met someone called Jasper. Jasper was a film director. He had made a short film about Lawrence of Arabia that didn't involve Arabia at all, was set in a small room in Winchester, but it had won some award in

Bulgaristan, a Silver Goat or whatever. Jasper was going places. Bit older than me. Arty job. Had a flat (a very small one) in Highgate. Managing low-ranking tennis players might be impressive for someone into tennis, but Vikki wasn't. I can't blame her for being smitten. We're all looking for a good deal. What we judge as a good deal. She didn't betray anyone. She didn't behave badly. She just didn't behave the way I wanted.

I did bump into her once not long after on the South Bank. On her way to a piano recital. She looked happy. She looked happy and delirious as if she had been at it all night and all day. I had lost. They say sport teaches you how to lose.

฿

There was an intermission. Of a few years. I worked on my plan for Graeco-Roman wrestling mania. I was having a good time. I wasn't having a good time. Famine and feast. The Violinist. The German Game Show Hostess.

I met the Violinist at a party. She appeared to be the only unattached female. I was desperate for a carnal carnival. Absolutely contorted. Nothing had been going right for months. It's funny how your standards just plummet when you're gagging for it. Maybe it doesn't reflect well on me, but I wouldn't have bothered if I'd had a shag the week before. She was wiry, didn't seem to be wearing any make-up, her skin wasn't ravishing, and she was wearing a terrible dress. It's easy to forget that some people dress badly, not because they don't care much, but because they have no money.

I threw in my piano recital knowledge, although it didn't make much of an impact. We agreed to meet for a drink, although she didn't seem very keen. But she turned up, although she looked deeply unthrilled. We had one drink and then, much to my surprise, she said:

"My place is just round the corner. Why don't we head back?'

I was so desperate I almost thanked her. Her place was a big old Victorian house that hadn't had any work done on it in a hundred years. A squat? She must have flatmates, I thought. I assumed we'd just head up to the bedroom, but she led me into the kitchen. Okay, let's be sociable, let's say hello to the gang before we get down to business.

They were in the kitchen, all sitting round a long, bare table. They turned to me as if I had been expected. The kitchen was as cracked and run down as it was possible to be, with a deep dinge. The taps had to be a hundred and fifty years old. The only bright note was one enormous, life-size colourful poster of a beaming Chairman Whatshisname on the wall, with some Chinese text underneath.

There were three guys, and six women. All of them looked like they hadn't had a decent meal in months. There's a smell to desperation and mental illness. I had noticed it with the Violinist, but I was desperate, and I hoped the application of cock would work wonders. Dr Dan to the rescue. A damsel de-distresser. That smell of hopelessness was really strong in the kitchen.

"Welcome, Dan," said a short guy at the head of the table. "Have a seat. We've been monitoring the international situation. Why don't you tell us how you feel about the international situation?" He was wearing some uniform, or something that had been a uniform a hundred and fifty years ago and was rather worn. Some cavalry officer?

"The international situation, yeah. It's something I monitor quite a bit too. Definitely needs to be monitored," I replied.

I had already worked out either I wasn't getting my oats at all, or there was going to be some ordeal before bedtime. One of the other guys in the kitchen was looking daggers at me, presumably because I had trespassed on his pussy patch.

"How much do you hate the government, Dan?" the leader continued.

"A lot," I answered because it was clearly the correct answer. And naturally I did. Although to be fair to the government, however rich their failings, however much I hated them, they weren't as barking mad as the occupants of the kitchen. The government, in comparison, were like my favourite uncle. It was me against a crowd, although they were all malnourished. Once, when I visited Trev's sister's, she and her friends had found out it was my birthday and a gaggle of girls had given me the bumps. I was surprised that they had managed to overpower me, and my erection had practically ripped through my trousers.

"We monitor the international situation very closely here," said the leader. "We're very concerned about it." The women all nodded in unison. "You're very wise, Sandeep," said one. The other guy was still simmering towards me. You're first up for a smack in the mouth, I thought. You are definitely getting it, if it kicks off. I looked at the door, wondering if I could just make a dash for it.

"How concerned are you about the international situation, Dan?'

"Very," I said.

"I'm so glad to hear that," the leader said. "There's good news though. What's the good news, Derek?"

"The Chinese workers and peasants are coming," Derek says. "They'll be here soon. The People's Liberation Army is coming to save us next year. We're doing our best to get ready to support them."

"Do you have any dental problems, Dan?" says the leader.

"Occasionally, nothing serious. The odd filling."

"The good news is that once the indomitable People's Liberation Army gets here, there will be no more dental problems. There will be no more health problems. All health problems, all illnesses, all diseases are the result of capitalism."

"Capitalism and their running dogs," Derek seconds.

"And don't forget about the universal justice," the leader adds. "Universal justice is only a few months away, Dan. Just hang on."

"Great. Good to know," I said.

"In the meantime, we're going to play a role game to help us understand the international situation."

"What could be better?"

"I usually play China and Derek usually plays the USA." The leader continues. "Dan, as you're our guest, would you like to be the Soviet Union or Cuba? Or perhaps the heroic Palestinian people?"

"Soviet Union, sounds great."

"Can I be the forces of clerical reactionaries?" the Violinist asks.

"You're always the forces of clerical reactionaries," says the leader. "I'm beginning to suspect you enjoy that. You're carrying a worrying amount of bourgeois residue on you."

"Listen," I say. "I didn't realize we would be doing some heavy-duty monitoring of the international situation. I hate to come to something like this empty-handed. Not properly tooled up, you know? Why don't I pop round to the off-licence on the corner, get a couple of bottles, some crisps, some nuts, so we can really get into it? Fuel up for a major session?" The prospect of something to eat caused a stir of approval. Even Derek Don't-Touch-My-Pussy-Patch, looked delighted.

As soon as I turned the corner, I legged it.

The Violinist phoned a couple of times afterwards, then gave up. I mentioned my narrow escape to Trev, who told me that the revolutionaries sometimes came into his shop, looked around and never bought anything, but never stole anything either. They tried to recruit Trev and assured him that the Chinese were only a few months away. For many years. Finally, one day, Trev said:

"You swore the Chinese would be here ten years ago, at least? So where are they?'

"Oh, they're here. Of course, they're here," said the leader. "They just haven't told anyone."

฿

Bitcoin wasn't even an idea.

One evening as I was walking past the Royal Festival Hall, I needed to take an urgent leak, so I popped in. As I left the loo, I was ambushed. "Hey, Scarface, were you here for the Clementy?" It was Vikki. I arrived unprepared. I considered a yes, but since I had no idea who or what a Clementy was, I played it safe.

"No, I was just passing through."

Vikki was there with a friend. We had some drinks. I tried not to stare at Vikki's breasts. The friend had to leave for North London, but Vikki was still in Brighton, so I volunteered to escort her to her train. Why not? In my coat pocket, I slipped on my Big Cousin's knuckleduster in case anyone took a fancy to Vikki's choker. We were chatting happily, apparently Clementy was some important piano botherer. It was late and when we got to Victoria Station we discovered that the last trains to Brighton had been cancelled. The wrong sort of midnight, whatever. No trains until the following morning. The Wheel. The Wheel taketh. The Wheel giveth.

"You can stay at my place," I offered.

She hesitated. "Just staying? Nothing more?" I nodded. I wasn't optimistic. Vikki had been shacked up with Jasper in Brighton for ages. I couldn't not offer the sofa. But as we went back, again, my spine was straighter, my stride stronger, I was hoping London was noticing that this woman was heading back to my place. Let them draw their own conclusions. Did Vikki make me a better person? Or did she simply make me feel like a better person? Is there any difference?

I thought it was funny that I'd finally get to spend the night with Vikki, but not in the way I had imagined. You do get some of your wishes granted, but there's usually small print. Not the way you imagined. The Wheel laugheth.

We had another drink. We slung some slang. I realized I had to try it on. I simply had no choice, otherwise I'd never forgive myself and I'd regret it forever. Just get it over with. She'll just say no in a kind manner. I was counting down to the expected polite refusal when she leaned over and kissed me. I kissed back. I cupped her left breast, lightly, but it was as if I'd set her on fire. With petrol.

"No one's ever kissed me like that," she said. I had been thinking the same thing, but this wasn't a time for marking. As I yanked off her underwear she said, "There's always something about that last bit of clothing, isn't there?" She was right. She laughed and said, "It's not a night for sleeping, is it?" She was right.

฿

No surprise, it turned out things weren't that great between Vikki and Jasper. He wasn't paying bills. They'd had the electricity cut off. Not because he didn't have money, but because paying bills didn't interest him. He was coming home late pissed as a newt. Not coming home for days. Been seen with lots of actresses, although none of his film projects needed actresses. They were all about brooding men in small rooms. Lord Nelson in a small tavern in Torquay, for example.

"Perhaps it's because he's mainly a brooding man in a small room," Vikki noted. "He just talks about money all the time. That he's depressed because no one wants to finance his films about men being depressed. He only comes home when he's depressed. That's where he likes to savour his depression."

In the morning, I ran a bath for her. "Let's share," I said.

"We can't both fit in this tub."

"I thought physicists knew about volume, space, how things

fit together, all that. I thought that's what you did for a living." I climbed in to join her, to scientifically demonstrate how two could bathe for the price of one. Even her breasts looked annoyed.

Once we had dressed, I offered to drive down to Brighton, so she could pack up her stuff and move in with me. She said nothing. I wondered whether she had heard my offer, but she was only two feet away from me. I didn't ask again because I didn't want her to say no.

"I'm off to the station," she said. "No need to come with me, I'm a big girl." I did get a big kiss.

฿

In my early twenties, the notion of having children terrified me. It was the end of everything. But with Vikki I now wanted the whole package. I wanted a daughter that looked like her, that had that nose. Was it Vikki? Or evolution prodding me to finally do my duty? You don't want to have a kid when you're fifteen or sixty-five, but otherwise I'm not sure there's a right time, you have to run the gauntlet.

It's the only time I had a backdoor relationship, and I didn't like it. I'm a front door sort of guy.

I was considering my tactics when Vikki phoned. "I'm moving to London," she announced. What? That was an unexpected present. I enjoyed the warmth of victory. It seemed natural. Winning seems natural in your younger years. "Jasper's got a job there. We'll be there next month."

My hope was that Jasper would just wither and blow away, like an autumn leaf. I kept adding up his misbehaviour.

"He's always late," Vikki said. "But always. But always unpredictably late. Will it be twenty minutes, forty or fifty-five? If it was regularly forty minutes, every time, like clockwork, you could work with that. Price it in, by being forty minutes late yourself.

How can a man be that late? We went to the cinema last week, I had to stand there waiting for him and missed half the film."

But no, Jasper didn't blow away, he was more like bubble gum on your sole. Vikki would turn up to my bed, and it's astonishing how extreme bliss makes you forget about anything else, any inconveniencies. I forgot about me. Us. It was Us. Us against the world. The world had no chance. That's what I felt. Something I'd never felt before. Total collusion. Vikki was grim-faced about Jasper's capers, but I couldn't get her to bring her wardrobe over.

She did bring a cripplingly expensive bottle of wine over for my birthday that Jasper had been hoarding, some French bollocks. I've never cared about the crew of flavours working in a bottle, and I suspect it was more about punishing Jasper because he had made her rewrite a script and then hadn't used it. "You're the writer, the auteur, I told him," Vikki snapped. "I stayed up all weekend because he had to show his script to someone on Monday, and I had to write a female character for him, because he's always getting criticism on how he doesn't haven't female characters or they're unconvincing. And then he cut it. I had my own work to write up that weekend.

"There's a test screening next week organized by Jasper's company, it's not one of his broody room projects, but if it's successful it should give him a leg up," she said. She was naked at the time and I was thinking the shape of her hips was like some naked woman I had seen somewhere, sometime in one of those famous paintings by someone famous. "Jasper asked me to round up some victims. Why don't you come and meet Jasper?" I didn't want to, but I couldn't look chicken.

The test screening was just off Leicester Square. I brought Parrish. The film involved a bunch of people in costumes, doing stuff that I didn't understand. They talked to each other, but it wasn't about anything. If there was a story, I didn't spot it. I was counting on some of the actresses stripping off, but they didn't. I wondered whether I had missed something, but I could tell when they handed out the questionnaires, everyone else was scratching their heads as to why on earth they were there. I was tempted to hand out some zeroes, but I stayed in the middle of the road for my scoring of the film. I didn't want to get into it with Jasper. Not then.

After screening, I met Jasper. I didn't feel outclassed. He was confident, pleased with himself and his new job at this big-deal film company. He rambled on about his latest project, George Washington in a log cabin in Vermont. Okay, points for glamorous, exciting job. He asked me if I could get him some Wimbledon tickets. Of course.

I had a stone, maybe a stone and a half on him. I was confident I could put him in hospital if I had to, and of course, I've turned your girlfriend into a sex slave. All in all, I judged I was on top, ahead on points, but he still lived with Vikki.

Vikki surprised me how nonchalant she was with me was. She stood there as if she had never seen me before. Her indifference was overwhelming. Unnerving. She left the pros behind. Women scare me with their pretence.

After the screening, as I chatted to Jasper, and Vikki, who was so elsewhere she might have been waiting for a bus, two women who must have been dragged in off the pavement from Leicester Square for the screening, came up to me.

"We're all alone in London. We don't know anyone in London. We need someone to show us around. You look like a real Londoner. Are you a real Londoner?"

This was directed at me. They weren't stray seventeen-year-olds. They had to be in their mid-twenties, overdoing the act of naïve-little-girls bewildered in the big city, to make it clear they weren't looking for directions to the Houses of Parliament or a recommendation for high tea. The one pleading for a tour guide was wearing one of those quarter-cup bras and a black see-through top that made you stare because you were calculating whether you were getting all the nipple or just eighty-five percent. Which I suppose is the purpose. That detail has lodged with me for free over the years. Her friend was leaning on her in an embracing way to make sure the message that they were one easily available package was clear. They were eager to get to work.

I'd like to state for the record that I rarely had women putting themselves on a plate, and this was the one and only time I was unmistakably being recruited for a threesome. In front of Vikki. If they had waited another fifteen minutes, Vikki would have been gone. I'm not sure I would have taken up their offer, because I was so smitten with Vikki. I would have preferred to chat with Vikki than to closely inspect the offered nipples. But it's surely bad manners to snub a threesome? Everything costs. Love costs. Love requires sacrifices. You arrive unprepared. I ushered the ladies over to Parrish who was getting into an argument with a hot dog seller. Jasper looked surprised, he had seen the ladies' message. Parrish never thanked me.

฿

I kept thinking Jasper will be jettisoned any day now. He'll go over some line. You could see the cracks. They were big cracks. If Vikki mentioned him, it was to complain about another domestic atrocity or romantic crime. But you don't live with someone for a couple of years unless there's something. Information rarely left Vikki, but once it slipped out; I think she had forgotten I was there. "Jasper was generous. He supported me when I was finishing my doctorate." I would have been generous too, but I wasn't there. When we were together, it was perfect. In and out of bed. Vikki and I never had the slightest dispute. As if we had been designed for each other. Would it have lasted like that?

One day Vikki phoned. "Jasper's going to LA," she announced.

"He's got some interview with some studio. He's sure he's going to get the job. That means moving there. He wants me to fly out with him."

I stayed cool. "You know my position. Stay. Let's get married. Kids. Dog. Lawn. Particle Accelerator. Whatever you want. Stay." She said nothing. She flew off.

A fortnight later in Las Vegas, she and Jasper got married. That was a real surprise. For all three of us. I was stunned, but I had no right to complain. No promises had been made or broken. In the end they probably regretted the crazy marriage in Las Vegas as much as I did. Many make the mistake of trusting marriage will improve the climate of their bond. It's the same as the week before.

But the USA looked a better deal than me. The prospect of work at the Livermore Lab, where they were doing the nukey stuff that interested Vikki, might have tilted the balance. We all have our goals, our dreams, our priorities. We all have to make decisions. Or the Wheel does. We're all human. I can't say she behaved badly, or at least any worse than I did.

I tried to pull myself together. Not very successfully. About a year later, I had a phone call at three in the morning. It was Vikki. "I just wanted to hear your voice," she said.

That's when I started coming up with reasons to do business in LA.

฿

The post office delivered my wife. One morning, the intercom buzzed. "Package". My flat was on the third floor of the building, so it was a long way down. What the postman didn't mention was that the package wasn't for me. It was for next door. I was tempted to say no, but the postman looked so defeated, I couldn't.

I had just come back from a session with the German Game Show Hostess. So plentifully beautiful, and tall. You felt you were getting a bonus that a short girl wouldn't provide. What twenty, thirty per cent more breast? As I pumped away, I took stock of the fact that I would never be with a more beautiful woman. Just not possible. This was the top. Men would only look at me with envy. But she wasn't Vikki. And there wasn't one thing I could say against the hostess, apart from the fact she wasn't Vikki. I was guilty about not being madly in love with the German Game Show Hostess, but I wasn't. Doing it doggy style has always been popular, it's very often the ladies' choice, but from a male perspective, it gives you time to think, to plan your world domination, to reflect on football, without your partner spotting your absence.

You have only so much time. Only so much emotion. Probably one uncontrollable love. Maybe you can have two or three deep loves. Hard to say. Four? If you're really hot-blooded and live long. You can't have ten. However much, it's limited. It's finite. Only so many goes. The game, the game ends. There have been some marathon tennis matches, but they end too.

I wasn't home much then. I'd be travelling or crawling back for a few hours' sleep, But the intercom went one morning, and it was the woman from next door looking for her package.

She was annoyed and not grateful enough for me looking after the parcel. I certainly didn't think this woman will be my wife. I didn't even consider trying it on. She was short and stroppy and had small breasts. Something that stood out when you've been doing a German Game Show Hostess. A few days later I was in the supermarket and saw her reaching unsuccessfully for some teriyaki sauce on a top shelf. I owe everything to inheriting a body of just over six feet. "You're quite useful, aren't you?" she remarked as I handed over the jar.

Is it the same for everyone? That truthfully life just happens to you? Your contribution is minimal. Optional even? I could have not bothered with that jar of teriyaki sauce.

I guess most men would admit that without their wife, they'd be dead. If you've had a long marriage, you know. You get so tangled up you can't live without each other. That I was travelling a lot helped. Many wives would be satisfied with occasional visits to keep an eye on the kids and regular cheques, so less wear and tear on the carpets and discarded beer cans.

I was starting to sink at the time I met my wife, post Vikki. For the first time, I felt not despair, but that everything was pointless. My job wasn't fun anymore. I had started drinking to knock myself out, for the first time. Men when they're in their twenties and thirties are close to invincible, but as they get older, they need propping up. Honestly, without my wife, I'd have been dead and buried long ago. "I don't want to hear another word about it," was her response to most of my moans at home. "Sort it or shut up." Whenever I see her in my mind, I see a look of investigation (what's he been up to?), or a look of reproof (oh, that). If you have found someone decent, and they are willing to put up with you, you've won.

"You're the only good thing in this world," I had said when I proposed to her. I'd thought about what to say a lot, I had wanted to say something memorable, powerful, true. As usual, my wife looked at me with suspicion. But she always did.

However, as I said those words I wondered if it was really such a great line, because if you are truly the only good thing in the world then naturally everyone will be queuing up to be with you. Of course I'm going to try to tie down, to capture, to hog the only good thing for myself. It's being selfish, not romantic. Maybe 'you're quite annoying, but I want to marry you anyway' would be the more romantic, flattering proposal. There's always friction. What you want in a spouse is someone you enjoy arguing with.

We had standard disputes that never ran out of steam. What is the correct number of toilet rolls to store at home? The bedroom window, open or closed? I was creating too much laundry. I was creating too little laundry. My wife was the one good thing

I found, on my own, that I earned for myself. That's what I say. Or did I? The Wheel?

I've been stumbling ever since her death. You can lose an arm or a leg in an accident, and that's it. I know I've lost parts of myself, and there's nothing I can do about it. The part of me that wanted to be a competitive tennis player, that wanted to bring Graeco-Roman wrestling to everyone's home, that's gone, it can't come back. But I can tell you one thing, unless you're in your seventies with terminal cancer, however dark it is, it can be turned round. You can go from nought to sought. Maybe you won't, but you can. The Wheel.

฿

"Who is Monak?" The Romanian doctor asked. I was puzzled, so was my mother.

"Who is Monak?" The doctor asked again. Eventually, I figured out she was asking who is the monarch, to see whether my mother was aware of her location in time. Although the Queen had been on the throne for so long, so no one was going to answer King Edward. But you have to hope doctors have some idea of what they're doing. I spent a lot of time in hospital with my mother, just watching her. Contemplating intelligence contemplating its extinction.

"If there's a question you want to ask me," my mother had said. "Now would be the time to ask."

Gary was away in Australia. My father was in too bad shape to go to the hospital regularly. He was tough. He'd been a boy soldier in the Korean War. He'd run a bookie's in Catford, and carried a cosh to work. But my mother was even harder. She wasn't good on following the world outside by this stage. What I learned was this. It doesn't matter whether it's Tuesday or Sunday, 1910 or 2010, if you're loved. Time doesn't matter if you're loved. Love beats time.

There are many parts of London I dislike, where I had to run for my life, Bermondsey, for instance, or where I had an unpleasant experience. I was run over in Kentish Town. My car was stolen in Kilburn. I was stood up in Croydon. I had never liked Hither Green. I didn't go that way very often, but I had always been ill at ease there, unsettled and I couldn't understand why. It was odd. Nothing unpleasant or remarkable happened. It was totally uneventful.

As I sat outside the Hither Green Crematorium, waiting for my mother's funeral service to start, I understood why. I had been sitting out there my whole life, waiting for my mother's funeral service to start.

You get a steady diet of disappointments. Someone said so, somewhere, sometime. As a parent you cross your fingers and pray you'll get away with it. You start off unable to choose between Harvard and Oxford for your kid, and you end up relieved your son's not a junkie. That my son got a job in insurance was hard to bear, but it's his life. You look back on your time, and there's not much there. You can sum up decades quite easily. When you look back. I lost Vikki. I met my wife. My parents died. My wife died and, to a large extent, I died. I lost my job. I stumbled onto crypto. I'm not all here. Two things come out of that.

"You what?" my boss said when I wanted to take time off to look after my mother.

The firm was angry. I was surprised when the firm was angry, not just short on the sympathy but furious, hopping mad with me when I wanted to take time off, unpaid, to look after my mother. Rosamund was long gone by this point. Obviously, I had zero respect for my boss, but I was surprised, not that he was so unpleasant, no, I was surprised that he was so swift to whip out the indecency, to wave it around. To flaunt it. I did consider filling him in, but that wouldn't have helped me, and I was wise enough by that point to know that his punishment was being him. Nothing worse than that, and no parole.

There's a lot of talk about luck for us crypto vets. Of course, we are lucky. I'm lucky that I'm not in a wheelchair and that my knob goes up. But those of us who made money, we worked for it. Took the risks, took the ridicule, had the patience. Get rich quick? It was very much a get slightly-comfortable slowly deal. But after that first twenty quid, I became obsessed, addicted to crypto, I spent all day researching, monitoring, relearning the old lessons, trusting no one and it wasn't all about watching the number go up. The ker-ching. It was a sort of revenge, a revenge on something, it was riding the future.

It's great going to bed and waking up with huge profits. It's not so great going to bed and waking up with huge losses. The Wheel. As it turns out, the new is old. Nothing older than the new. Just as you tend to turn into your parents, your father or mother, although you think you won't, crypto became the same. I'd like to say I was resilient, strong, but I wasn't. I was three-quarters-crazed. Stumbling. You just stumble along, arriving unprepared. Stumble on.

฿

Bitcoin was around three thousand dollars. Soup changed everything.

I put a piece of paper into a large metal bin. That's how it started. A bit like throwing a crisp packet into a bin. The piece of paper was a twenty-pound note and the large metal bin was a Bitcoin ATM in Old Street. I had stopped for some soup and the café had a Bitcoin ATM in the corner. No one was using it. It looked very unused.

I'd seen the machine the week before. Maybe I should buy some Bitcoin? Just dip my toe? See how it worked? I had downloaded a Bitcoin wallet onto my phone over the weekend. Then thought, no, this is stupid. I'm fucked enough already thanks.

But I felt like some soup, and the ATM was still there. I couldn't help feeling I was throwing the twenty quid away. Acting casual, before I fed the note into the ATM, I had looked around a couple of times, to make sure no one I knew could see me. If I was making a fool of myself, I didn't want any witnesses.

I did get a paper receipt as if I was buying a sandwich. Bitcoin was an elegant con at least. I was glad no one knew what I had done, so no one could actually laugh at me when my twenty quid rode away over the hills and far away. It was hard not to feel like a mug, a simpleton, someone who's been done. All that. A volunteer chump at my age.

I tried to play it cool. I tried not to immediately check the bitcoin wallet on my phone. After twenty minutes, nothing. The billing says the bitcoin confirmation cycle is every ten minutes. My arse. Almost nothing you're told about Bitcoin is true. After thirty minutes I had made peace with the loss of my money. After forty minutes, I checked the wallet and it had arrived. I owned some bitcoin. I felt triumphant. I hadn't been shafted. A result. That's how grim things were for me.

They say you're lucky. No. There's some graft, there's some bottle involved. This was 2016. Ming had told me about Bitcoin earlier, but I hadn't paid much attention. Then, one night when I couldn't sleep, I was watching some nutter on television who was gabbling on about Bitcoin. He was doolally but his argument made good sense. But as anyone selling something knows, rational arguments are good, but emotional ones are the killers. "If you want to make the banks cry," the nutter said, "if you want the banks to go boo-hoo-hoo, buy Bitcoin." That was the moment I decided to buy some bitcoin.

Bitcoin. It shouldn't have happened. It couldn't have happened. But it did. One man, probably, and his code, one man and his laptop, in a kitchen, coughing up industries and trillions all over the world in little more than ten years, it's absurd. Implausible to the max. Un-fucking-believable. Preposterous. More bonkers than bonkers. All that. Something out of nothing. An incredible amount of something out of nothing. Although that's how the universe started, so I'm told.

Is it merely a long con? Is Bitcoin just a mighty payday, or have I gatecrashed one of the great moments of history? Up there with the enslavement of fire, the invention of writing, the power of flight. A moment everyone will be pointing to for thousands of years, as long as there are people to point. And Dan was there. Bitcoin rulz okay?

Not that it matters to me either way.

If I'd got into it in 2014, I might have made more. Really bulging bags. But then I might have been tempted to cash in too soon. Those who got in then couldn't believe their good fortune. They sold to buy a bike (second-hand), a car (third-hand), to put down a deposit on a flat (small one). They sold to buy a pizza. By 2016, the game was already different. The stakes were looking serious.

In many ways, I started as a caveman. My wife called me that often enough. When I was a kid, I was an aspiring hunter-gatherer. Catford's not the greenest part of London, but there was mud, nettles, bushes, trees, conkers. Nature's generosity. Pulling someone's trousers down and throwing them onto a bed of nettles. Branches, ideal for whipping and torture. We made our own entertainment. Bombsites. They still had those.

Now I live in Dubai. In the way that anyone lives anywhere. Now. Do you live anywhere? We mostly live online. It's what I reply to the question "where do you live?" I live in Dubai, as new as it gets. Nowhere newer. They made it a couple of years ago. I have enough Arabic to get into trouble, but not out of it, so I hardly ever use it.

I have bags of crypto. My bags are big. Some of the crypto is boring. Bitcoin, well, it's boring now. It's not going to melt your face. Dull. But dull has its uses. Dull gets a bad press. Bus drivers have Bitcoin now. But I do have a couple of exotic, futuristic, long-shot, quantum-resistant cryptos. Or at least resistant this week. For a laugh. And I have a starship engine in the corner, under the bed.

฿

Where are those stories of everyone living together happily? The stories stop at happiness. We're told that happens sometimes, but we don't get the story. Take Paradise. If we had Paradise, the next thing out of our mouths would probably be: "More Paradise, please." Or "Could you top up this Paradise a little?"

We had paradise once, they say and then someone came along and messed it up. That's world history. It was great, or good or at least okay and then someone came along and messed it up. When I was five, we had a trip to the seaside, I spent a whole afternoon building a sandcastle, a masterpiece. A naked toddler just ran through it. The most annoying thing was that he didn't do it deliberately. He was just running around not paying attention, discovering motion.

BITCOIN WAS THIRTY thousand dollars or so.

The first time I met NotGuilty he was in the hallway, singing a song I didn't know, but which had the refrain: "Who might your hole-provider be?"

NotGuilty was in the hallway with a brush and dustpan, sweeping up some bits of packaging that had been dropped there, almost certainly by our French neighbour, Jasmine. Jasmine was unbearable in a variety of ways. She was always having all-night parties, a confirmation of her unpopularity. If you're popular, you go to parties, you don't throw them.

NotGuilty was probably unique in that he was the only person I knew in Dubai who didn't have a cleaner or maid (and his place looked like the cleaner had left five minutes ago). The building's maintenance staff would have cleared up Jasmine's debris within a day, but NotGuilty was there with a long-handled brush and pan. It looked wrong, like a dolphin playing badminton. NotGuilty's manner suggested he should have a sawn-off shotgun, a crowbar or heavy dumbbell in his hand, not a long-handled brush.

"Everyone calls me Not." We shook hands. I found out about the full version of his name later.

It was a bit peculiar as we sized each other up. He was suspicious when I told him I grew up in Catford. Then he thought I was winding him up. Then he grew suspicious again as we established that we had walked the same streets for years, gone to the same shops, we knew some of the same people. Chiefly the criminals, like Kev. He had gone to the other school in Catford, but otherwise our early years were a perfect copy. But neither of us could remember meeting. It seemed impossible.

"I come from a large family," he said. "I had six brothers and sisters. When I was ten, I ran away for two days. No one noticed."

Eventually we discovered we had both been in the cinema the evening of the pitchfork incident, when someone had been skewered with a pitchfork halfway through *Rocky*. The ambulance crew had a hard time getting the victim out of the seat.

"Where do you get a pitchfork in Catford?"

"That's what I thought," said NotGuilty. "Bit theatrical. Bit desperate. A bit look-at-me. Probably some Millwall fan keen to get noticed."

Until the mushroom business, we didn't have much to do with each other. I checked up on him. It was even weirder that I hadn't come across NotGuilty, because he was quite a celebrity. Certainly in legal circles. Lawyers, policemen all knew him. NotGuilty was on first-name terms with most of them. Most of them saw it as a game and went home and forgot about it.

He had dozens of charges and court appearances: armed robbery, murder, assault, theft, money laundering, drug dealing, kidnap, blackmail, arson, abstracting electricity, counterfeit money, you name it. All with the same result. Not guilty. But when he was acquiring his nickname, I was spending most of my time out of the country, nannying tennis players in Australia and the US. LA a lot.

"I didn't ask for this, you know," he said.

I had gone to lunch at Obligatory Julian's. Naturally, like everyone else I didn't want to see Julian, but he sometimes had interesting guests at his lunches. He knew he had to, otherwise no one would turn up. The lunch was a disappointment, but you have to gamble now and then. Julian usually had a chef to do the honours, but this time he cooked himself. I slung some slang, I ate, I left. His mushroom risotto was tasty, to be fair. Julian's place wasn't far from mine, so I walked back.

I had got in the habit of using the stairs to go up the three floors to my flat. Sometimes I even have a little trot. It was my gesture to keeping fit. I go to the gym now and then, but really now and then. I can't be bothered. But I've made using the stairs on the way up a rule. A habit. I was feeling poorly by the time I got to my building. Definitely off-colour. I should have got in the lift, but because I wasn't thinking clearly, I found myself, out of habit, on the staircase, so I thought I might as well walk up now.

Your body knows. Your body knows when it's ill. And then it recognizes the next level when you're seriously ill. And it knows when you're dying. Most people know. My mother called me when she knew she was going. That day.

By the time I got to the first floor I wasn't ill, I was seriously ill. Then I started vomiting like never before. Like I'd been saving it up all my life. NotGuilty found me unconscious. He never used the stairs. But he had seen Jasmine waiting for the lift and chose the stairs.

The previous Saturday, I had been woken up by a rowdy party with vicious dance music in Jasmine's flat at four in the morning. I went over to complain.

"But I'm just having a few friends round," she said. "Surely I can have a few friends round? They're actors. It's not a party. I mean, I haven't had a party for months."

"You had a party last Saturday. Remember, I came round to ask you to turn it down a little at three in the morning?"

My polite complaint wasn't getting anywhere I could see. Jasmine actually seemed on the verge of laughing at me, when suddenly she dropped the smirk. I turned and saw NotGuilty was standing behind me. The look on his face terrified me and I wasn't even the target. A look that said amongst other things, you're very, very lucky there are witnesses about. I was angry, but NotGuilty was way beyond that. A thousand years of rage were queued up behind his eyes.

"Okay, we'll turn it down a little." Jasmine shut her door hurriedly.

So NotGuilty had seen Jasmine waiting for the lift and had been afraid he would snap and pummel her if he was in her company for even a few seconds. He chose to walk down and found me out of it on the stairs.

They told me at the hospital when I came to, I had been about fifteen minutes away from complete organ failure. Not that you can trust anything a doctor says. They love to up the drama. Their wizardry. But two of Julian's other guests were there. Maybe I beat the Wheel that day. Or NotGuilty and I beat the Wheel. Or just business as usual for the Wheel.

Somehow that cemented our relationship. I had no choice but to be grateful to NotGuilty for saving my life. But in a strange way he was grateful to me.

I got lots of tales of dodgy doings. He never said I did this or that. It was "I heard", "They say", "Someone I knew." "A friend told me". Or "My mate Harvey." "My mate Harvey" told him a lot of things, so much so, that I assumed Harvey was an imaginary friend, working as a pronoun. NotGuilty's mate Harvey talked a lot about the Brink's Mat robbery. A lot. Almost every time we met.

Brink's-Mat was the biggest gold robbery in British history (and probably the last big one, Crypto will replace all those cumbersome chunks of metal). I checked up on this and they never found out for sure who the robbers were. One or two might have got away. For someone who wasn't involved in the Brink's Mat robbery, NotGuilty talked an awful lot about it. And knew odd, small details, that I checked up on later, that were true. He was either there, or was really pally with the robbers.

Of course, he should have something more than a one-bedroom flat on the same floor as me if he had been a party to that venture, but it's ironic that the most successful robbers were pretty much robbed themselves. As NotGuilty commented: "That's the trouble with criminals, isn't it? That they're criminals. Maybe there's some honour amongst thieves, but there's also a lot of thievery." Of course, the most successful weren't that professional. The Brink's Mat bunch didn't know the gold was there. They had come for some currency. Bits of paper. They stumbled on the gold. The Wheel took them up, and then brought them down.

About a month after the mushrooms, NotGuilty knocked on my door, carrying a parcel.

"Dan, I'd like to ask a little favour."

It was what I'd been dreading. I suspected something like this would happen. It's funny how "I'd like to ask you a favour" can be pronounced in a way that it sounds like: you owe me.

"Small favour. Very small favour. No fuss. I want you to look after something for me."

What is it? Drugs? A gun? A human head? NotGuilty doesn't have to harp on the mushrooms to get my yes. I know myself well enough that much as I want to, I can't say no. Gratitude is one of my failings. Not that NotGuilty put himself out for me really, he hardly went the extra mile. He was walking down some stairs to avoid thumping an irritating French woman. Made a phone call. It was good while it lasted.

NotGuilty unwrapped the parcel and produced what looks an odd-shaped pink stone, almost egg-shaped, larger than a football. Well on the way to being a boulder. The would-be boulder had some dark veins. Maybe some exotic mineral? It had a polished sheen. It was the sort of doorstop that someone in advertising would have in their penthouse loft. Arty. Conversation piece.

"Yeah, Dan, I'd like you to look after this. Don't, er, don't leave it lying around. Best thing, best policy, stick it under your bed, or put it in a closet."

"What is it?" I pick it up. It's incredibly heavy. It's rock solid whatever it is. Some ultrahard glass? "Is it a doorstop?"

"Always work as a doorstop, isn't there? Just something I don't want lying around in my gaff.'

Right, so whatever it is, it's hot. So hot it might burn through my floor. It's something people are looking for. People that worry NotGuilty, so people to very much worry about. But I don't know what it is. That's not much of a defence in court, but it's a start. And if NotGuilty is worried about his door being kicked down (although I did notice his door was much more door than mine, a confederation of locks and metal), I'm probably safe because no one but us knows it's here. And if someone does kick down my door, they can have it, no palaver, because I'll have done my duty.

After NotGuilty leaves, I go to the computer and try to find out something. I spend a couple of hours looking for stolen art, strange pink rocks, weird pink stones, bizarre pink boulders, bespoke doorstops, all that. But nothing fits the bill. I wonder if I can find someone, pass the buck, just in case my door does get kicked down. Why doesn't NotGuilty put it in a security deposit? You'd need a supersized one for this thing. And also, NotGuilty knows. Vaults. Vaults are where you keep valuables. Vaults are where you look for valuables. Governments can get into them legally. And then he knows people who can get into them illegally.

Bury? You can always bury your loot in some out-of-the-way place. But you can never be sure that someone else won't turn up in the most isolated place with a spade. A detectorist. Or someone else wanting to bury something or someone. Someone will come along and mess it up. I decide not to worry. His mate Harvey will probably explain what it is. For someone who can't keep his mouth shut, it's incredible he's never done one day in jail.

Four days later, NotGuilty reappears and asks for the rock back. I'm delighted to hand it over. A couple of weeks after that he's back on my doorstep with the rock. "No, it's better with you," he says.

฿

I drive an old Citroën. A small one. It belonged to someone's maid.

I love that the Lambo and Bugatti drivers are peeved just by me being on the road. I'm lowering the tone. Apart from impressing the easy-to-impress, I've never understood sports cars. If you're a motorhead, into torque and waxing, and love long-distance drives, okay. But unless you own a race track, or you live in some remote part of Arizona, the best that you can get is a second or two of acceleration. I love the Lambos rocketing past me, and then me pulling up next to them at the red light. Eye contact is a must. In Dubai, like everywhere else, driving a car translates to sitting in traffic. Okay, sitting in traffic, in sunshine.

The Citroen is also easy to park, although there's plenty of room at Ming's place.

You don't choose your parents. You don't choose when you're born, where you're born. Do you? You don't choose your schoolmates. You don't choose your neighbours. You don't choose your colleagues. Doesn't leave much.

Some things, you can attempt to choose. Have a go. Your job. Your wife. Your car. Your friends. But how much of the choice was yours? And did you botch it? How much is everyday botchery? The Wheel is in charge. The Wheel turns. Can you beat the Wheel?

I definitely chose the car and I'm claiming at least half of Ming.

Ming buzzes me in and I admire yet again the rai stone in his driveway. Apart from the cost of lugging a huge chunk of limestone around, how do you get a rai stone? Do you give the Yap embassy a call?

Ming doesn't have to worry about anyone stealing it, because not much gets stolen around here. The blessings of a police force that will kick the shit out of you and make you eat maggots. They still have punishment here. Troublemakers fitted up.

Fantastic. What have human rights actually done for you? Lately?

No, the rai stone isn't going anywhere, it's so heavy. And no one around here knows what it is. It's a crypto joke. Me and Ming, we're crypto lifers. We're crypto geezers. We make crypto jokes. That lump of limestone was money once in Yap. Stone age cash. Money? Money is what is considered as money. I suppose the rai stone might be mistaken for some modern work of art, that's the only risk.

I read somewhere that the word rai might mean whale, and let's face it, if anyone's a whale, a crypto whale, it's Ming. What am I? At most, a crab or average lobster in the crypto ocean.

"Dan, I can't believe you still have that," says Ming. "You're having a laugh with that car. I hope the neighbours mistake you for the plumber. Now, you have to try this Chablis."

"How are you?"

"Fine. A Professorship at Cambridge would have been nice, but life here's not bad. I can't complain."

Always that ship that escapes.

Ming's wearing a T-shirt. A Kalashnikov rifle emblazoned with a Bitcoin logo and the slogan: "Bitcoin – There is no negotiation". What a lifer. What a crypto brave. I don't make much noise about it, but for Bitcoin, I would fight to the last bullet. Ming really cares about wine and pours me a glass of Chablis. He doesn't ask me about the bag I'm carrying.

Smoking or drinking, I never got into. From my youth. I pulled pints for others, and I like to think I have an honourable mention in the development of the cocaine trade in the UK. However, I thought abstaining would help my tennis. It didn't.

I was fifteen when I started doing shifts at the Inner Space Exploration Club. Hardly anyone knew it was called that, since the whole point of an illegal drinking den is that you don't have a big sign outside with a name. There was a tiny sign perched behind the bar that said Inner Space Exploration Club in psychedelic script, but no one ever noticed it. It was Archie's joke. Or something. Archie who ran it, had been a hippie like Trev, but had given up on it almost immediately. Those who knew about the place just called it Archie's.

My Big Cousin worked the door sometimes. Not that there was any trouble. The illegal dens were for those who worked odd hours and couldn't catch a lock-in. Mostly tired cleaners and security guards, unpopular prostitutes. Imagine the worst pub you've been in and go down a notch. There was almost no choice of beer or crisps, and you paid more. The card games were for money.

Was my father worried that I was working in an illegal drinking den? Not at all. It was a different era. He was pleased I was acting like a responsible adult, earning my way. He knew I didn't drink or smoke, because I was already on my way to being a tennis pro, which he thought much odder than working in an illegal drinking den at fifteen.

"How's the Chablis?" Ming asks.

"Monstro."

I play along with Ming. That's the thing about making it. You need toys to fill the time. Waiting for the Reaper. Waiting to be reaped. Ming has a wine cellar that would put most Parisian restaurants to shame. So they say. To give shape to the day, I still timidly trade a little crypto. A little. Because with all gambling, in the long run, you lose. Who makes money in trading? Year in year out? Those who teach trading. The fluencers. It's the gold-rush shovel phenomenon. Sell shovels. Whoever said that.

"Anyone called you lucky today, Dan?" asks Ming. "I was insulted with the term this morning. I'm not going to tell anyone ever again I'm in crypto, I'm so tired of being insulted like that."

"Well, we are survivors. Although, as a survivor, I don't have any survivor's guilt."

"A moment's silence," says Ming, holding up his wine glass.

"A moment's silence for all those crypto braves who didn't make it. For the fallen."

"For the fallen."

"For those who spunked it all on SafeMoon. Or other digital degen disasters. For those whose wallets were hacked."

"For those who left everything on an exchange," I add.

"For those who left everything on an exchange. For those who exploded into smithereens because they aped on the leverage. For those who lost their keys. For those didn't make enough money for their wives to open poncy, money-munching, pointless art galleries full of purple tosh. Unfathomable amounts of purple tosh."

"That was a lot of purple," I agree. Evidently, Mandy's not at home.

"You slumming it with Pepe?" Ming asks. "Are you degen-ing it? Has your face melted at all?"

"I'm only here for the tech," I say. It's an old crypto joke, but if you only play it once in a while, you can get a chuckle. Ming obliges.

There's always the shiny new coin. You need to get some before it hits the big exchanges. By the time the shitcoin hits the big exchanges and the tourists, the picknickers, the day-trippers, the toe-dippers, the mindfulness coaches, the housewives and the shoe-shine boys are lobbing in their money, it's too late for the life-changing gains. You might do okay, but you're near the blow-off top. And the more likely outcome is you're left smouldering like a neglected bonfire. Although hardly anything disappears completely. Nothing 'goes to zero'. It can be cosying up to zero, but there's always the hardcore. It's like the music business, once you're in, you're never out, you're only playing tiny venues to tiny, elderly audiences.

"Pepe? Leave it out," I say. "Complete bollocks."

"We all know that, but have you shamed yourself?"

Trading's simple. It really is. It's simple. Devastatingly simple.

Buy low, sell high. That's it. It's an unbelievably simple formula. But where exactly is low, and where exactly is high? And buying low, not that hard, but you can also buy something that's taken a vow of lowness.

Pepe is guaranteed useless. Even in the coin category clearly marked self-confessed-we-must-insist-you-understand-how-useless-we-are meme coins, Pepe will be waving madly at you. There are no circumstances, no outlandish events, that will ever allow Pepe to cross the border into the land of the useful. It's completely anti-value.

On the other hand, it's easy for the useful or the valuable to lose it. With a shift of time or circumstance. A tankerful of oil now, big money. In say, 300 AD if you're in the Amazon jungle, not much benefit to you. Having a powerful semi-conductor as you watch the chariot races with a mad emperor in Rome, less valuable than a grimy crust of bread. Golfclubs in the Jurassic.

Gold's done well. Gold would get you stabbed just about anywhere at any time. Gold, the bandit-magnet, the killer-caller.

Because, when you've solved the problem of getting it, when you have it, you have the problem of keeping it. Keep your bags on a crypto exchange, you can lose it all as the exchange goes down. And many an exchange has gone down with all hands. Keep it yourself, okay. Don't lose the seed phrase for your wallet. Don't let others get the seed phrase.

One of the things I learned in business is give people what they want, or at least attempt to give them what they want. Give them something that maybe from a distance looks a little like what they want. I'm amazed that people leave their real seed phrases on cards marked seed phrase. I have cards marked with seed phrase, and I leave them in fairly obvious places, because if someone really wants to break in, they will. You can't stop them, but you can appear to give them what they want.

I have cards marked seed phrase. Take one, please, because, it's not my seed phrase, it's a nonsense seed phrase. I bought thirty books. I might read them one day. The seed phrase is hidden, there in those books, in a deceptive way. If you're that good, and I doubt anyone apart from a team from a national intelligence agency is good enough to crack it, you can have it. You deserve it.

Hardware wallets? I keep a couple of shitty old Ledgers, subtly placed in cubbyholes. Please take them. There are no bags on them, so after you've spent days with sophisticated software cracking them, you've got sod all. The only thing I'd say for a Ledger is that it's easy to fit into your Khyber in an emergency.

I rely on a Trezor Model T, probably the final word in crypto wallets, this week, that will look like an embarrassing penny-farthing within three years.

I keep it on me, most of the time, in case I need to leave fast. And although I'm a lifer, an old school crypto geezer, ducking and diving, yes, I do keep some stuff on exchanges, the two biggest on the basis that if they go down, all of crypto will probably go down. And you know what, back in rainy London, I have a bank account. Yes, they will cause you misery in several ways, but you have the modest consolation that they won't be causing you misery deliberately. Just a smattering of traditional old-fashioned cock-ups and dimness.

"I've just sliced a deputy minister of defence this morning," Ming announces. "L2, L3 work, tinkering."

Every now and then Ming does an operation to keep his hand in. Unsavoury regimes have grown fond of Ming, although as he explained to me, you have to be careful. If you operate on someone like the ruler of Equatorial Guinea, a ruler who actually crucifies his critics, that is with real wood and nails and hammers, you might come across someone at a North London dinner party who peddles human rights, who knows about Equatorial Guinea, although it's low in the indignation charts, and you risk placards jostling outside your practice. But no one cares about the junior ministers.

"They usually turn up with a gold ingot or Swiss francs," Ming says. "This was the first patient to pay in crypto."

"What did he use?'

"Eth. I paid the anaesthetist with it too. Adoption. Adoption."

I'm surprised Ming even bothers invoicing. Whatever a spinal decompression or discectomy costs, it's a lot less than the freight on the rai stone outside. It's the toying that's the charm. But Ming's right. It's good to see the spread of crypto. To see that the message is working. I sip my Chablis or whatever it is.

"I was chatting with the deputy minister beforehand," Ming continues. "He was proudly telling me they don't have censorship in the Congo. He was very insistent on telling me, that there's freedom of the press and no office of censorship. Censorship involves so much work, he says, what with social media and so on. Then he elaborated. Every year, a journalist gets kidnapped, tortured to death and the body is left where it will be found and universally acknowledged that the journalist was tortured to death. Guess what? No one wants to be that journalist. How's your undercarriage, by the way?"

"Okay. Nothing new. Business as usual."

Ming did me too. A long time ago. I never liked going to the doctor, I'm not sure why. My GP was curiously unconcerned by the fact I wasn't able to walk properly, but eventually I splashed the cash and made my way to Ming's office.

He looked at the scans, told me I had hardcore stenosis, explained I needed an operation, talked with some glee about the many horrible things that could go wrong with the operation to clear up my spine. Then since I had mentioned I was in sports management, Ming asked me if I could get him Centre Court tickets at Wimbledon. Could I? As I wanted to walk again and have my knob in working order, I was happy to help out.

The firm. It was the nature of the firm that I only had a decent salary towards the end. I never made much money, but the perks were good. I did get to travel the world, mount German Game Show Hostesses, rampage through room-service, and get massaged a lot. I could also lay my hands on tickets, something I took advantage of.

Instead of hustling me out of his office, GP style, Ming invited me for a coffee next door and a chat and to see how I was on boxing matches and the luxury suites at Chelsea. It was the first time I'd hear about Bitcoin.

"Do you hate banks, Dan?" he asked. "And what about governments?" He told me about Bitcoin. It sounded interesting, but I'd didn't pay much attention. Ming was already up to his neck in it. Hence the readies to import a rai stone. He had his son deep mining Bitcoin and Eth on his school's computers. No one had heard about mining then. Certainly not in schools. No one gave a toss about the electricity bill. It was a different era.

"We got back the school fees in a few weeks," Ming explained. "It was like inventing bank robbery."

We'd both have a major obstacle course of problems shortly afterwards. Ming would have to leave his hospital job because he had raised concerns about his colleagues killing patients. No one wants the truth.

"The truth is an awkward shape, it never fits in anywhere neatly, there's always an awkward bit sticking out for someone to trip over." No one in management wants to hear that they're not managing properly. Then his colleagues retaliated by trying to bump off Ming's patients when he went on holiday. All stuff you don't want to hear. Ming hopped to an exclusive private practice.

"Are you looking at anything?" Ming asks. "I see you as my in-house prophet. I tell everyone Dan was right. You were right about Luna. You were right about FTX. You were right about the bow-wow coins."

I was right about the bow-wow coins but for the wrong reasons. I thought they were stupid. But the herd loved them. The herd gets a bad press. You need to be mooing with the herd. There's no upside to being on a mountaintop by yourself. You don't want to be at the front of the herd, you'll go into the ditch. You don't want to be at the back, everything will have been trampled or eaten by the time you get there.

The best traders have sapped their emotions, no attachments. Very much like the most successful people. No strings. Nothing holding them back. But they're unlovable. That's the worst thing that can happen to you. That you're unlovable. You have to love to be loveable. Although loveable comes with occupational hazards. Love costs. The price of love is pain. You can pay at any point. I don't admit to Ming that I'm not a prophet. It makes him happy.

"Haven't been researching much, because of various reasons. The mushrooms etc."

"Yes, that caused waves."

"I'm in reasonable nick since the mushroom business," I say. "I haven't been near a doctor for months."

"That's the best thing, Dan. Never go near a doctor. They are lethal. Above all, never be alone with a doctor if you can avoid it."

"How can you avoid it?"

"I don't mean seeing a doctor professionally at a surgery or a hospital. No, some misfortune there would be awkward, and your enemies might sniff around."

"I don't follow."

"Doctors can bump you off and bump you off in a way that means they have an excellent chance of getting away with it. They'll be probably signing the death certificate for a start."

"But why would a doctor do that? Don't doctors want to help people, sometimes?"

"Think about your competitors. Think about it honestly. How

many of them, if they had the power to off you, with safety, with impunity. How many of them wouldn't have progressed their career by offing you. If removing someone gave you an advantage."

"But if your patients die, isn't that a bit of a dampener on your career."

"I wasn't talking about patients. You're right. That doesn't help. I'm warning you about not being alone with a doctor socially."

I reflect I'm alone with a doctor, socially.

"They might off you for a wheeze to feel like God. I mean I could have spiked your drink, you wouldn't know," Ming continues. "You'd croak, I could take your key go to your place, clear out your crypto, take a trophy. Grimly announce you had all the classic symptoms of a stroke. The general public don't appreciate how many apparently healthy individuals, often youngish individuals, drop dead every day because of a lurker in their ticker or noggin. And how often we don't know for sure why someone signs out. We don't know much. We know there are major organs, the heart, the liver, the brain, because they're hard to miss. But it's embarrassing how little we know."

Does the Chablis taste okay? I don't really know how Chablis should taste, where the borders are. I can't be arsed about wine. Wine tastes like wine. Like gin tastes like gin, and whisky tastes like whisky. And vodka tastes like vodka. Was that odd note, an eccentric grape or death? How do you know if a wine is good? It's one of the more expensive ones in the supermarket.

How well do I know Ming or anyone? I know he's helped patients, non-patients, been indiscriminately kind with time and cash, but what does that prove? A clever cover? Nothing guarantees anything. I mean, nine times out of ten I could tell you what my wife would have responded to something. I know she couldn't stand mushrooms. She'd practically climb on a chair if she saw one. But there's always the tenth time. Ming got me into crypto. Friendly people go mad too. It happens every day. Is

Ming winding me up? Prankster. They always say, "I'd never have thought him capable of that. I can't believe he did that."

"Are you going to the party?" I ask so I don't think about how closely inspecting Ming's floor might be the last thing I see.

"How could I not? The event of the year. I was planning to go to Shanghai to see the cousin and some colleagues, but I postponed. I tell you, those boys out there, they're really pushing the limits. Totally off the books larks. I mean if you want a licence to kill, or just maim, a medical degree is the ticket. But we're so tame in Britain now. You want authentic mad scientist, threat to humanity capers, atrocity in a lab, Shanghai's the place. They scared me. They turn you into a half-pig, or hollow out half-your-brain and then charge you a fortune. That was Mengele's only serious mistake, he didn't charge his patients."

Ming was always talking about his cousin in Shanghai; when Ming was young, they actually sent food parcels and underwear to him. Now his cousin owned the seafront, and Ming was desperate to catch up with him, so he could brag at weddings and funerals.

'What about the promise, that whatisname . . . er . . ."

"Hippocratic oath? Come on, Dan. Everyone from antiquity onwards thought Hippocrates a pest. Do no harm? The only way you can do no harm is by doing nothing. Noth-ing. I was looking forward to seeing my cousin in Shanghai."

So much of life is pretence. Pretending you want that job. That you like people. That you're tough. Clever. Whatever. That you're not gutted completely by your wife's death.

"Medicine's a brutal business," Ming continues. "My professor, when I was young and green, told me a story about his batty neighbour who ran a mini cat shelter for distressed moggies. These cats were forever coming into his garden to do their business, killing birds, disrespecting the aquatic life in his carefully curated pond.

"He explained the old lady came round to his place one

Saturday for a sherry just before Christmas and sadly passed away. Peacefully. 'Sad but peaceful.' He smiled as he told me that it was sad. He was teaching me something, or maybe he was bragging, but I think it was a trade secret. Part of an oral tradition, a secret tribal initiation, a blessing passed from mouth to ear. You are allowed one or two hits, you know, when's someone's really interfering with your garden."

"What, he knocked her off? You honestly think so?"

"He didn't wink. He didn't actually give me a conspiratorial wink and a thumbs up. But I'm pretty sure he did. I remember thinking the sherry he had given me tasted a bit funny. He didn't like me, he didn't seem to like anyone, in fact, so I was worried that he was taking me into his confidence only because I was never leaving the room.

"There are occupational bonuses, like you being able to get tickets, there are some bonuses for all the whingeing you have to put up with from patients. I'm sure the old trout had been cremated by this point, or I doubt I would've had that anecdote. So many neighbours would have resorted to poisoning the cats, week after week, laboriously erasing them piecemeal one by one, but he took the whole shebang out with one sherry. Daughter sold the house, no more marauding cats.

"It's like your tax returns, you can always get away with one or two fast plays. That's what I mean, you should never be alone with a doctor. As long as you don't touch the money, because that's mostly the motive for murder, as long as you don't get too cute, too omnipotent and put too much icing on the cake, the police will never suspect, or even if they do, the plods aren't good enough on metabolism. Harold Shipman could have been six hundred, not out. Stick to what you know. His mistake was forgery. Again and again."

Ming pours me another glass. "Monstro Chablis, you're right." I express approval of the Chablis, although I couldn't tell it from any other wine. And even if I could, I don't care. Make others happy when you can. Almost always a waste of time, but it costs nothing. In many ways I'm dead. Waiting to be reaped. Agreement is a bad habit from my management days, elementary manipulation and ingratiation.

But you've got to get excited about something. Ming's wife opened an art gallery. It's one of those things you do when you have a bit of money and time, open an antiques shop or open a quaint restaurant, or an art gallery because you know, artists are more spiritual than chefs, although you do get more than one chef trying to be Zarawhathisname, and the benefit of art is that it keeps better than locally-sourced artichoke or even wine.

I toy with coins, which to most people would be much weirder than caring about grape-juice or landscapes. I'm toying with some AI coins, which is the fashion this week. You have to be quick with this stuff de jour, because it really only lasts a few weeks or months. Defi, GameFi, Yieldfarming, metaverse, chonk coin, fuckcoin, these are bubbles, but you can have some fun with the nonsense coins.

I also have a small bag of sceats. A real bag, a leather bag, with seven sceats. Ming has his rai stone as his crypto punchline, I have the sceats, small silver coins from the dark ages, as mine. It amuses me to think someone in London more than a thousand years ago, the dark age me, someone would have valued these coins. Used for food, for sex, for status, for murder. The carriers are gone, evaporated. It's no use digging up people, but the money's ready to be unearthed for another tour. The money remains. Hard, hard, well-hard money. A long-standing joke. I love the designs on them.

Of course, there are those who will tell you that there's no use for crypto, and what that tells me is that you know nothing about crypto. Of course, most crypto is rubbish. Duds. Cons. Most of everything is rubbish. Most politicians are rubbish. Most films are rubbish. Most GPs are rubbish. Most pizza is rubbish. The list goes on. I can't be sure which horses will finish, but a few of them will. I promise you that. Places your bets, and of course as always, with the favourites, well, the returns are less.

"You thinking about AI?" asks Ming. I don't think too much. If AI takes over the world, honestly, I'm not bothered. Could things be worse run than now? I'm waiting to be reaped. If there's a nuclear war, not that bothered. It's selfish, I know, but it's hard to get away from that. Poisoning's not that bad. Obviously, you won't enjoy it, but it's quicker than cancer. A few minutes or hours of distress. You won't know it's coming, so less distress, less fussing, less panicked attempts to put things right.

Either there's a big plan, so I'll be redirected somewhere, or there isn't. I'd like to say thank you to my parents, to my wife, to my son, to my friends, to Vikki's breasts, to a German Game Show Hostess. Thank you. It could have been much worse, but I'm tired and I'm waiting to be reaped.

I worked hard. Work doesn't work, really. Not working doesn't work either. I made a point of being early to meetings and not showing annoyance when others sauntered in twenty minutes late. You always hope that the laggards would somehow get punished, but usually no. I swallowed a lot of rage. I answered every call, letter and email, even when there seemed no benefit. I gave it the works.

It's very debateable whether that helped. Beat the Wheel. Can you beat the Wheel? I suspect many people like you more if you treat them shabbily. I survived in a tough business. I just wonder if it had anything to do with me? In the end?

"I'm dabbling in AI," I say. "But only dabbling. To pass the time. The era of face-melting gains is probably over. You get that once, you can't reasonably expect it again. You should just say thank you."

"But why be reasonable?" Ming points out. "Although you're

probably right. Our faces will never be properly melted again. And your wife only needs one art gallery, after all. We don't need bigger bags. We don't need the fabled laptop of South London."

"The what?"

"The fabled laptop of South London."

"Sorry?'

"You know, the fabled laptop of South London. The Catford computer, as some call it."

"No, I don't know."

"Everyone knows about that."

"I don't."

"Yes, you do. Everyone does. I must have mentioned it several times."

"Not to me."

"Wasn't it you who first told me about it?"

"No, it wasn't."

"Come on, you know, the legendary story, the one that got away, the myth, a story so perfect it's unlikely to be true."

"So, tell me."

'It's been knocking around for years. A story so good maybe it comes from the collective unconscious."

"I'd like to hear it."

"It's a tale of crime," says Ming sitting back in full storyteller mode. "Crime and punishment, the hell of failure, the torment of what could have been. A mugger mugs someone, takes his rather worn laptop, sells it in a pub for the price of a couple of pints. But soon after the mugger finds out he's the mug. He's been done, he's stitched himself up like a kipper, because the laptop was bulging, bloated, bursting with bitcoin. It's like Satoshi's stash. The laptop had enough bitcoin to change the world.

"Thus, the mugger had every crook, and non-crook in South London, London, hunting for the laptop, the laptop that could change the world. The game changer. The ultimate reset. Unbitch yourself. The Catford computer, it's your terroir, supposedly, I'm sure you mentioned it once.'

"No. Crypto. Vast fortune. Catford," I say. "Those are areas of interest me. That would have been something at the top of the remember list."

"Okay, I'm telling you now. It was the God-strength fortune. The mugger went mad with regret, so they say. Topped himself."

"I can see holes in that story."

"It's a legend. Like Atlantis. Or El Dorado. It's not my legend. I don't have shares in it."

Ming has been very restrained. Finally, he asks: "What's in the bag. Your bags?"

"It's what they call an imposition."

I take out NotGuilty's boulder.

"What is it exactly?"

"I don't know. But I was hoping you'd do me a small favour and look after it for me."

"It looks like something Mandy would have in her gallery. If it were barmy boulder week. Are we talking something dodgy here?"

I shrug my shoulders.

"You can say I told you it's a present I bought for my other half's birthday," I suggest. "And I don't want them finding it beforehand. Full deniability."

I'm not going to be left holding the boulder when whoever kicks down my door. My mustard's still fresh. Ming loves intrigue. He'll like the idea of a bit of the nefarious.

"I'll stick it outside next to the rai stone," Ming says. "I can always say someone dumped it."

฿

Destiny. Destiny called once. Destiny actually called me. Beckoned me over. Destiny Jones. Destiny was a headhunter. Who called me. Is that your real name, I wondered, or a front you came up with so you would be remembered? It worked. Destiny wanted to meet about an opportunity. We arranged to meet.

But Destiny chose me. We all want to be Destiny's pal. Destiny has a reputation. Destiny gets results. You learn quick that sitting on your backside, waiting for the lobster thermidor to fly into your mouth, doesn't get you very far. But we all fancy the idea of the Big Moment. The Big Moment loitering for us, out there. Just out of sight. Round the corner. Taking a last puff on a spliff-break before hoving into view. That's it's inevitable. And the best part of inevitability is that you can sit on your backside, because it's inevitable.

"You'll need every penny you earn," my father told me when I was a kid. I didn't pay any attention because I knew I'd be a zillionaire by the time I was twenty-one. Small island of my own. Maybe two. No worries on how. It was all under control. Inevitable. Like winning the lottery. Like crypto.

Destiny didn't turn up. I sat in the restaurant for more than an hour, waiting for her. Then because I was hungry, I went round the corner to a much cheaper place for a bite. I found out later she had left that headhunting company. Never heard from her again. Or any headhunter.

There's the stunts that you do. Your rackets. Your jumping up and down. Your banter. Your pleading. Then there's the stuff that falls out of the sky. Your supporters? Your back-up? Fewer than you think, more than you know. Someone said so, somewhere, sometime, didn't they?

฿

Bitcoin is thirty thousand dollars or so. To get to Bigger's party, we go up to the sixtieth floor.

I muse on the coincidence that it's my sixtieth birthday.

Destiny? Are you calling again? Is this a message? I haven't mentioned my birthday. I don't care about it and don't want anyone fussing with a card or buying some knick-knack that will go into a black bin liner when I croak.

My bags are big, but I have little interest in material things these days. Apart from a bite to eat and a comfy bed. That's as mortal as I get. That's as earthly as I am. Someone up there has a sense of humour. There is comedy out there, like ozone, moisture and carbon dioxide. Levels vary.

There is no security in sight when we get out of the lift. But it must be around. A Gurkha is occasionally spotted.

"Wow," says Artemis. "It's an official wow."

"That is the correct answer."

Bigger's place is big. It occupies four floors of the building.

I've only been here a couple of times, and I, who broke my wife's heart because of my disregard for décor, and okay, tidiness in general, I've never been anywhere so clean, so new.

So gleaming that I was afraid of touching anything because it was so perfect. It didn't look like a home. It looked like a museum that had just opened. You wanted to stand in a corner and exhale lightly so your breath wouldn't cloud anything. There had been trays of modified radishes and olives, decorated with delicate spirals of hummus or I don't know what, so carefully arranged, that although I was hungry, I didn't dare to touch the food and ruin the presentation. It would have been like taking a massive dump on the floor.

But the place is heaving tonight, so I will go wild with the canapés and other goodies. I can't see Ming.

"Evening, Dan. Good to see you," says Obligatory Julian.

Obligatory Julian is in attendance, because, yes, he's obligatory. You'll always find Julian standing next to the most powerful person in the room. His shamelessness is so world class, if it was a sport, I'd manage him. Since Julian is not standing next to

Bigger, it means Bigger isn't here yet. I also admire Julian for not feeling at all embarrassed about almost killing me and his other dinner-guests. That's some insensitive insensitivity. He deserves to be in a government somewhere. I doubt he senses that I'm blanking him.

There's a large Bitcoin counter, showing the price in elegant numerals as it twitches up and down, minute by minute. No one here is going to be worried by a shift of a few dollars, or even a lot of dollars, least of all Bigger. It's a mix of art-work and a joke.

NotGuilty is standing by one of the food spreads, shovelling in the oysters. I'm not sure why he's here, because he has nothing to do with crypto. But it's predictable that he's muscled in to the party of the year. He sees me with Artemis and his mind starts whirring. My life and past are endlessly fascinating for him. Always asking follow-up questions like an interrogator aching to crack a cover story. I'm curious how he will handle this. And how Artemis will.

"Artemis, let me introduce you to my favourite neighbour, Not. Not, this is Artemis."

"Sorry, is that as in K-N-O-T?" Artemis asks.

"Nah, it's not as in not guilty," NotGuilty says.

Is he going to wheel out the NotGuilty spectacular? He's noticed Artemis's breasts, exactly like her mother's. Whirr, whirr. He's wondering is this a long-lost daughter or niece, or some juicy secret I've been hiding from him? I'm not quite as dull as I've been judged? Into sophisticated escort services? And whether he can gain admittance. How that would affect the neighbourhood? Whirr, whirr, whirr.

"Is that really beluga, beluga caviar? I've only ever seen spoonfuls of it." The mound of caviar on the table has caught Artemis's attention, and she hasn't realized that Not is the short-form address of NotGuilty, temporarily blocking NotGuilty from unfolding his origin story.

"Beluga galore. Tuck in," NotGuilty urges.

I've never been able to take caviar seriously since Parrish started feeding his lottery ticket. He played the lottery regularly for a while, correctly identifying the lottery as his only hope of getting his hands on big money. He'd go into town and steal some caviar and feed it to his lottery ticket, by smearing it onto the ticket. He somehow thought that introducing his ticket to luxury would work, giving it a taste of wealth. There was no tradition of witchcraft or the occult in his family, and Parrish wouldn't have been able to read about it, so he deserves credit for coming up with the idea.

It didn't work, but I have to say for a while I did wonder whether he was on to something, that he might beat the Wheel, and if I examine my own behaviour, his feeding a lottery ticket was no more impractical than some of my own delusions. Or buying Bitcoin.

"I won't have any," NotGuilty says. "I had a bad trip with beluga. Not going to lie, I don't even like to look at it." Don't ask him, Artemis. Please don't ask him.

"Oh, what happened?" Artemis asks. It seems like the polite thing. Here we go.

"I was at Zurich airport, doing a friend a favour. I was at the gate, about to get the flight to Dubai, right, when I get a call." NotGuilty takes a step back for dramatic effect. "They're waiting for me. I'm told that they're waiting for me at Dubai. Now, I had a bit more cash on me than was strictly allowed, I was doing this friend a favour, and I didn't want any complications here, as it's so cushy, so I think I'd better get rid of it quick.

"The airport had one glam jeweller's. Great. Pick-up a swanky watch or two, a gold chain, right? The shop was closed for renovation. However, there's a fancy caviar stand. Okay, I'll have some of those pricey fish eggs. The first hundred grand's worth was quite tasty, but then I got queasy. I bet they still remember me in Zurich. The staff at the caviar bar were ecstatic. Service included. I bet I'm a legend. At Zurich airport at least. They thought I was mad, but like a mad Santa Claus bringing them a month of Christmases.

"But I still had a lot of cash, and it occurred to me that if they're waiting for me in Dubai, maybe they're watching me here now. What if they'll pounce now? Caviar makes you a bit paranoid, I reckon. I thought about just dumping it in a bag in a bin, but airports are crawling with cameras, so they could track me down. I rush over to the bogs and start flushing the extra cash away, like a maniac. Say what you like about the Swiss, maybe very tidy, but their toilets are feeble. It got blocked. Those big notes are tough. Then I bunged the rest in the hand towel bin. But I had to get my flight, they were calling my name all the time by this point. I've never been able to look beluga in the eye since."

NotGuilty had told me that story a couple of times. It was the first and last time he had transported cash.

"Were they waiting for you?" Artemis asks.

"No."

Some of us have no sense of humour. Some of us are willing to face a little ridicule for the delivery of a good anecdote. I don't think NotGuilty has a sense of humour. All the proper villains I've known, the pros, the fully qualified, none of them did. Muggers, burglars, gangsters. Some of them believe they have a sense of humour, but they don't. They believe they're loveable rogues, they're not. Tell me that hilarious story about you mugging that milkman again, Kev.

Humour requires a bit of humanity and real villains lack that, because someone always gets hurt. NotGuilty does enjoy attracting satellites, so he doesn't mind raising a smile or two to do that.

I doubt Artemis can spot in NotGuilty's eyes, as he gives us the caviar yarn, the motorcade of rage in the distance. You need to know him for a while. In certain lines of work, you're not surprised by a brief, anonymous, unidentifiable call. You have to act. NotGuilty believes the call was a practical joke. I know because in the less funny version of Zurich airport he gave me, he's hissed about it at length, looking for the person who made that call.

"Business or pleasure? What brings you to Dubai, Artemis?" asks NotGuilty. It's time for the interrogation, so I excuse myself and go over to Math Cat who's eating a hamburger in a corner on his own. Bigger is a thoughtful host. Math Cat has never been seen eating anything but hamburgers, so hamburgers he gets. From McDonalds.

There are three notable things about Math Cat. My wife regularly described me as dressed like a tramp, the victor of the worst-dressed award in any homeless shelter, because I hung onto some loyal shirts and trousers. Math Cat would have made her so angry that she would have started beating him without a word. He does look like, and is dressed like, a scarecrow. Do scarecrows get work these days?

His girlfriend is a stripper. High-end, who does some burlesque and show-dancing too, but regularly pole dances internationally at the top joints letting her labia see the world. It's one of the major talking points in Dubai. Why? Why? Why does this outrageously attractive, witty woman live with Math Cat? NotGuilty bumped into her sunbathing on a beach one day. "I couldn't help myself, Dan. I really couldn't. It was unfair, she had it all on display. Not going to tell a lie, I had no choice, no choice but to rush home and knock one out. Why Dan? What is she doing with Math Cat?"

Money? No. You could blindfold yourself, throw a dart and hit a millionaire in Dubai, one with a tan, a six-pack and slick conversation and a desire for travel. We all accept that Math Cat is friendly and is kind to animals etc., but he hardly ever leaves home and only talks, haltingly in a post-spliff way, about hamburgers, his unhealthily large collection of Fall bootlegs and Bitcoin, or more precisely, the technical analysis of Bitcoin. I doubt he's ever combed his hair, which manages to stick out in at least four different directions. Why?

Technical Analysis has been described as astrology for men. It's maybe a bit better than that. Self-fulfilling prophecies. Head and Shoulders. Descending wedges. Bear flags. Trading is like poker. Stay zen. Don't get involved with your bag. Don't date it, don't hate it. If you've done your homework, and you're cautious, use low leverage and you're up against noobs who haven't done their homework and are rambunctious, you get a steady income.

The problems. You do get emotional about some bags. Wedded to some. I actually find it hard to sell my Bitcoin. I feel so grateful to it. I long Bitcoin, never short it. This is more like a crusade, than business. Then, events. Events can blow away TA. The world can just trample it. And another major risk: getting high on your own supply. You get some success because it's a bull market, suddenly you're not a trader. You're a genius. You're the ruler of the world, the greatest product of homo sapiens. Then the market reaches into your nether regions with a clawed hand, your intestines are pulled out and burned in front of you and no one wants to talk to you. It's like doing coke. Stick to the occasional snort.

There's a problem about asking Math Cat about Bitcoin. I don't want to ask him about Bitcoin today, because I know what will happen.

"How's the burger?" I ask. Math Cat nods approvingly. He swallows. For a moment, he reflects on the mouthful of hamburger that went down. He doesn't reflect on the bit of hamburger that fled and is now nestling in his trousers. "I've got a great new soundboard recording of a Fall gig in Croydon," he says. "Much better than the last one I gave you. Let me burn you a copy."

"Thanks." I haven't been able to bring myself to tell him I can't stand the Fall. I'd sooner listen to pans falling out of a kitchen cupboard. And that I don't have a CD player. Does anyone now apart from Math Cat?

I can't help myself. I can feel the urge to ask about Bitcoin rising in me. Maybe this time will be different. But I know what will happen when Math Cat opens his mouth. People are predictable. Well. People are predictable, until you need them to be. Then not so much. "So," I ask. "How's Bitcoin?" And here we go.

"The interest rate hikes . . ." Math Cat starts. The problem about asking Math Cat about Bitcoin is that with all his charts, monitoring of the media and macroeconomics, he knows too much to be able to answer. Or perhaps, to be fair, after an hour or so, you can't take another instalment of answer. You can't fit it into your nut. What you want to know is, is it worth bunging in a few grand? Math Cat won't say yes and he won't say no, but he'll say everything in between.

Artemis comes over, having escaped from the incredible anecdote machine that is NotGuilty. "The two hundred day moving average could go up," Math Cat is explaining. "It could go up, or depending on what the Fed does, could go down. Or possibly just stay in the same zone, depending on . . ."

I introduce Artemis to Math Cat. She opts not to comment on the hamburger. "What about our host? Are you guys going to introduce me to Bigger?" Artemis asks.

I should. Although she'll find it disappointing. They say Bigger knows Satoshi. Or he's told them he knows Satoshi. That he went bowling with Satoshi. But Bigger . . . he's a bloke in a provincial boozer. He dresses almost as sloppily as I do. He's not just tubby, Bigger looks soft. You fear your finger could sink in several inches if you prodded. You'd guess he was solving computer glitches in local government, some failing secondary school, not Silicon Valley.

Would I choose to spend time with Bigger? On the basis of his personality? Probably not. Even with his crypto lore, he's veering into being boring and unfunny. But like many weedy lab mice, maybe he has a vicious streak. You'd assume that the lab mice who've been tormented frequently would value peace, love and harmony, but some are only itching for their turn to dish out the cruelty.

The gossip is that, apart from collecting bins of bitcoin like popcorn, long ago, when I was bumping into Jasper in Old Compton Street, he's done some heavy market manipulation in trading, destroying all sorts of positions. Ruining people. For laughs.

"His art is . . . not something you see every day," Artemis says. "I've counted a Courbet, a Cézanne, a Gauguin, probably a Monet and some De Stijl, Die Brücke and Bauhaus spin-offs. Juvenilia, minor works, or as the man in the street would put it, no good, but all together they could get him something that would make everyone go Oooh, a jaw-dropper, like a respectable Picasso or Van Gogh. I mean I've only seen most of these works in dusty books. It took me a while to recognize them."

Artemis studied fine arts. I didn't and that's why I've never noticed them. Paintings are like curtains, or shelves, for me. A table. Or fire extinguishers. Something in the room. A painting is something you put on the wall. Like wallpaper. Something popular in a place people want to call home. Most of the paintings at Bigger's are of trees, bushes. I've never understood paintings really, or paintings of trees. If you want to look at a tree, why not look out the window at a tree, or if you have the money for a posh painting of a tree, why not plant some trees of your own?

"I can't make up my mind," says Artemis.

"About?"

"About whether it's more annoying that he's spending his money with discretion, so as not to commit a vulgar assault and battery with his wealth. That he's whispering he's a cognoscente," Artemis says. "Or is someone buying it for him?"

"You'll find the Picasso in the toilet," says Math Cat. "One of the toilets, I can't remember which one." Artemis laughs. She might have trouble finding the Picasso. The facility I used was so large I was almost exhausted by the time I'd covered the distance from the door to the bowl.

My guess is Bigger buys art himself. He's hands on. The suggestion that he's an art expert? I don't care. I can recite all the winners of the FA Cup since 1871. So what?

Back in the twentieth century, we carried this thing called memory. It was a different era. Bigger's only leaving hints lying around? That surprises me. There are three Bored Apes hanging on a wall, but that's more, I-have-so-much-money what do I-do-with-it? and also showing he's with the kids. Like those parents who ask their kids at dinner about the music they listen to, not because they care or want to like that music, but to show they're up to speed, that they're not hopeless fossils.

"Although juvenilia is still juvenilia," Artemis says. "They're not that good. I'd sell them all and get one no-nonsense show-stopper."

Perhaps that's it. I remember Bigger saying, "We were all shit once." That it's a learning process. That greatness is preceded by not-greatness. Maybe those pictures are a subtle chuckle about evolution, about struggle, about courage, a tribute to optimism. Seems a bit poncy, but I suppose we all have a pinch of pretension lurking, some variety of vanity.

I only buy cheap clothes. That's a sort of pretension. Unflashy vanity. That a cheap label is in no way inferior to an expensive label. I scoff at your glitz. I wear twenty-year-old t-shirts. I don't tell anyone that, but maybe I like the idea that someone will notice.

I'm wearing a Mickey Mouse watch. It's a Mickey Mouse watch made in Hong Kong. Not Mickey Mouse in that it's shoddy (okay, it was a cheap, mass-produced watch). It's a genuine Mickey Mouse watch with Mickey on the dial. From the seventies. Or maybe even the sixties. It's the only possession I have from my childhood. My uncle Steve was in the Army, came back from

Hong Kong, when it was junk headquarters, and gave me and my brother a watch each. Although as the older brother, Gary got the hands with glow-in-the-dark luminous paint. A big deal at the time. In the final clear-out after my father's death, I found mine in a drawer. My father had kept it for some reason.

I almost didn't wear it. Would it be condemned as irony? Dubai is a place where your watch acts as a sort of spokesman for you. I don't know why this is, but anyone who isn't involved in the watch business, who has a collection of watches, a stable of watches, who treats them as holy relics, is an arsehole. This is a guy thing. One fancy dazzler, why not, if it makes you happy? You might acquire three or four over a lifetime. But collecting watches? Talking about watches? Unapologetic watches? Collecting watch straps? Changing your watch strap with your fucking outfit?

You have to watch it with the watches, with all the trinkets, toys, the paraphernalia, the decor. Be careful. Beware the pleasure of treasure. Don't become the property of property. A thing of things.

To my surprise, the Mickey Mouse watch worked. It had had a good kip for the better part of half a century, but still. I wear it because I genuinely don't care what anyone else thinks. And it says something. Not sure what entirely, but it says something. Cheap junk, granted. Well battered. But it works. Still in the game. It says that.

I've noticed Artemis has appraised it, but hasn't commented. And Mickey also says: you never know. You never know. Who's going to make it. Who will last. Someone said so, somewhere, sometime. I've got an ostrich strap for it, because it is ridiculously expensive, probably two hundred times more than the watch's worth. So definitely ironic, and somehow sums up my life. Unglowing hands to ostrich strap. Hope my life doesn't carry on like that, that it's not as circular as the watch and I'm back with Mickey.

I was disappointed when I discovered that there are genuine vintage Mickey Mouse watches from the 1930s in America, that are skilfully engineered and worth some money. Some Iraqi stopped me in the mall and quizzed me about my Mickey knowledge and clued me up. Maybe Artemis thinks it's one of those Americana treasures.

I'm probably as heinous as the label-worshippers that parade in the malls. Harder to detect or condemn though. Showing off, by not showing off. Swapping one vanity for another.

"That safe," Artemis says. "It's not solid gold, is it?"

She's finally got round to the gold safe. It's a big safe, not one of those mini-safes you get in hotels, in the middle of the floor we're on. It's impossible to miss and possibly another Bigger joke. The inside-out safe. The gold on the outside, and the not valuable stuff inside. Or a brag that there is something more precious than gold concealed inside. You choose.

"I haven't had it tested, but Bigger says it's solid 24 carat."

"Yes," says Math Cat. "If he's not conning us, you're looking at about one percent of the world's gold supply. You can have a go at Bigger's competition, but don't forget you're only allowed one guess."

Math Cat has beaten me to the punchline.

"What competition?" Artemis asks.

"Bigger says that if you can guess what's inside the safe," I explain, "you win the safe. But everyone only gets one guess."

"Have you had a go?"

"Not yet."

"I tried," says Math Cat. "Bearing in mind who Bigger is, I thought it might be the Bitcoin White Paper. All that gold would be an appropriate shrine for that sacred scripture."

"How do we know you weren't right?" Artemis asks. "Is there any invigilation?"

"The terms and conditions are a little vague," I say. "As terms and conditions always are, especially as the terms and conditions here don't exist. We only have Bigger's word that the safe is solid gold, and that if you guess correctly, he'll fess up."

"Maybe it's Satoshi's bowling ball," Artemis says.

Math Cat nods. "That would have been my second guess. I suppose I could come back with a false beard and fake ID and have another go." Artemis is studying Math Cat now, although I can tell her courtesy is preventing her from giving him the lecture about getting a haircut and burning his clothes.

"Has anyone kept a list of guesses?" she asks.

"The punters, no. There's a pad on the safe where you can enter your name and your guess. I've had a look at it a couple of times, so I saw the recent entries."

"And they were?"

"The safe is a mirror. Your guess says more about you probably, than Bigger."

"But what were they?'

"Rubber duck. Your ancestors. Half a ton of steel. Come on, let's see this evening's crop."

We go over to the safe. The latest entry is from NotGuilty. "A comic" is what he's written. It's a slightly surprising guess, but a clever one. It's always the stuff from your childhood or youth that you value most. Is there anything after the age of thirty that really shapes you? That goes deep down. Maybe even twenty?

Did NotGuilty go to that fantastic comic shop in Lewisham too? When I was eleven and I went there and saw an almost unimaginable number of comics, it was paradise, just as when I was sixteen, the club was paradise. Then Vikki. Do you see a pattern?

I've been pondering having a guess in Bigger's game. Knowing Bigger, I could imagine it would be something pretentious. Something that would make him look like a pusher of profundity, although I can't imagine him handing over the safe if I were right. My guess is there's nothing inside. Nothing.

"If I put 'something' would that be cheating?" Artemis wonders.

"Just cheeky," I say.

Something can't be nothing. Unless it's a turn of phrase, a dismissal. Your bag is nothing. But not pure nothing. Is nothing something? In a way it is.

"Where's our host? Can you see him? Why aren't you introducing me? I need to appraise him," Artemis asks.

"You'll be disappointed," I reply. That's one of the things that you learn as you age. The world isn't run by geniuses. Wise-cracking gurus. Colourful sages. Inspirational rebels. Wily megabrains. The great aren't that great. They're individuals who've stumbled onto the controls or a bag of gold. Someone said so, somewhere, sometime. Things are run by people like you. With odd hobbies and strange skin complaints. And little patience.

I only know one big cheese from when he wasn't a big cheese. From way back. We played a few times when we were kids at my tennis club. I can't remember much about him except that he was in a constant hide-and-seek battle with his mum over his porn mags and that he was worried that his girlfriend didn't have enough pubic hair. It was a different era.

He became the billionaire that billionaires felt had too much money, and owned half of Richmond and some mountains in Switzerland. I was surprised when I heard because it didn't seem right that I'd know someone so famous and successful, however vaguely. And I suppose he was important because he was about one per cent of the nation's GDP. Was he clever? Yes.

But not that clever. I never thought, yes, he's so clever, he's bound to bend the Bank of England over and give it a good seeing-to. He never succeeded in hiding all the mags from his mum. Was he motivated? Yes, he wasn't any better than me, but he did run hard around the court, fought, but most everyone did. I don't think anyone at the club would have put money on him as a future international puppet-master.

"You will be disappointed," says Math Cat. "Bigger isn't here."

"He's not at his own party?" Artemis says.

"He had something urgent, apparently. Back in Europe. He didn't want to cancel the party. Everyone looks forward to it so much." Math Cat opens another McDonalds carton and examines the contents. "Do you think he really went bowling with Satoshi?"

"Maybe he's bowling with Satoshi now," I say.

"Do you guys know who Satoshi is?" Artemis asks.

"There are three or four lead candidates," says Math Cat, before sinking his teeth into another cheeseburger. "Maybe five. Or six?"

"I have an educated guess," I say.

"So?"

"It doesn't matter. It's like whatshername's box. Bitcoin is a brilliant invention but -" I start.

"But Satoshi, blessed be the name, didn't really invent anything," Math Cat interrupts. "Satoshi put together things that hadn't been put together before. He saw things that others didn't see. That's the genius."

"Genius is just hard work," I add. "Someone said so, somewhere, sometime. Proof of work. Satoshi opened the door, or blew it open, if you want to be more revolutionary. But he, or she, or they, whoever, was right to walk away. Maybe this will all be forgotten in a few years." I wave at Bigger's home.

"The world is full of collapsed palaces with stray dogs shitting in them. Or maybe Satoshi will be one of the big names in the history books. If they still have books after we're gone. But it's like Whatshisname that shot, you know, Thingamajig who started the First World War, he became a footnote who sat out the war in a comfortable jail while others froze to death in trenches."

"But Satoshi's a hero to you guys," Artemis says. "Wouldn't it be a big deal to meet him? Her? Them? They say you're not supposed to meet your heroes. I met David Bowie once. It was fantastic. He was so sweet. I got his autograph."

"I met him too." Why couldn't I stop myself?

"Where?"

"South London. It's a small place."

"Did you get an autograph?'

"No."

Bigger isn't here. That's some magnificent party throwing. Throwing without being there. That's power. Making them dance, pulling the strings without even pulling the strings. Puppet-master mastery. I feel slightly like a pet monkey. It's not so bad.

Cedric brushes against Artemis's leg and Artemis jumps high.

Artremis's got moves. But then you don't expect to have a black panther cuddle up to you. I could have warned Artemis, but I like my fun too. Cedric has all the dynamism of a beanbag and lies around most of the day, something I have to concede I do a lot of. Given the opportunity.

For a black panther, for a major predator, Cedric's ridiculously friendly. Although they say animals are good judges of character. I've known house cats with more attitude. He likes to be scratched and it's only occasionally when he jumps upon a table, or leaps from one floor to another, does something pantherish, powered by millions of years of evolution, that you see how much more professional and powerful a big cat is than your household mog. It's the sort of thing that can make you believe in God, because it's unnecessarily beautiful. There's no need for that level of grace.

"It's tummy-scratching time," I say.

"Isn't this illegal?" Artemis regards the prone panther waiting to be scratched.

"Unethical, that whole area? That is the correct answer. And somehow contributes to climate change. This is Dubai. This is Cedric."

"Cedric?"

"Wouldn't have been my first choice for a panther. I guess it's another of Bigger's jokes, but I don't get it."

"Yeah," says Math Cat analysing some Bollinger belts on his mobile. Morsels of hamburger are on his trousers. "Respect for the carnivore. How bout Reaper? Stealth. Death. Hell? Too metal?"

"Claw?" suggests Artemis.

"Claw. Paw? Pow?" Math Cat continues.

"I like Pow." Artemis scratches a blissful black panther. It's not a bad life being a pet, if you get the right gig. The unloved gold of freedom.

"I'll suggest a name-change if I see Bigger."

I spot Ming talking to a woman on the other side of the party and go over to say hello.

"Dan, have you tried the beluga yet?" Ming says.

"No."

"Dan!" exclaims the woman and beams at me expectantly. It's evident that we know each other, but as I work her face, there's nothing I can cling onto. She's in her fifties, well-turned out, pleased with herself, but what else would you expect at Bigger's party? Is this someone I slept with in the Jurassic? Please give me a clue.

"Dan," she says. "It's me. Gina." It takes me a moment to digest this. Even with that information I can't really recognise her. Her hair is different, and she has a deep tan. Fortunately, Gina's so thick she can't sense the horror thrashing in my insides.

"Dan's the man who gave me the start in my career," she gushes. "I owe it all to him."

"Gina, what are you doing here?" I manage to ask, because I have to ask something.

"I've just started working for Bigger. Helping him with admin, you know, keeping the Gurkhas in line."

I manage not to laugh. I'm also not that angry. In my youth I would have been outraged that she has this soft, doubtless well-paid job, but now I know it's the natural order of things. The Wheel at work.

"So, how are you, Dan?" Gina says. "I heard years ago somewhere the firm let you go."

"Yes, they were very upset that I wanted to look after my dying mother."

I ask Gina six or seven questions to create the impression of being interested in her, while I count down to my exit. I fire the final question.

"Bigger's not here, is he?"

"Oh, he is," she gives a smile, meant to be enigmatic, but which declares I know something you don't. Not surprising since she works for Bigger.

"We must meet up for a drink, a proper catch-up drink," Gina adds.

"We must."

I return to the Math Cat and Artemis huddle. Math Cat has acquired another hamburger and is talking about quantum computing and its possible threat to crypto. Artemis hasn't inherited her mother's love of physics and looks adrift. How does Math Cat stay that thin, gobbling down burgers? He doesn't even look like he has room for three burgers in his body. Does he just eat at parties? Once a year?

A man-sized robot slouches over to us. I thought it was just some exhibit, some conversation piece, the weird expensive junk the rich like to litter their palaces with, but it's alive. Or moving.

The robot moves stiffly, but smoothly enough to be disturbing. When I was a kid, robots were a joke. They were large dustbins, with a tape-recorder to issue catchphrases or motivational quotes. Clunky, overlarge versions of dolls. Later on you'd get alleged robots working in restaurants and cocktail bars. Simple, repetitive tasks, that they'd still mess up. What they are now scares me, honestly, because you can see where it's going. I'm glad I won't be around when it comes to the battle.

"Hallo Dan, Math Cat," says the robot. The robot's head is

mostly a screen, suddenly showing Bigger's smiling face, his features blending in well. He chuckles for a moment, knowing I'm gob-smacked. That gives me a moment to regroup.

"Bigger, sorry, mate, I didn't recognize you without your body. Is it in storage? Are you having it frozen?"

"My dangly bits are on a trip to London. Who's your charming companion?" Bigger asks.

Youth, beauty, brains, hard to go wrong; but, you can. Artemis's dress is so perfect, she must have ironed it ruthlessly before coming out. It shouts: tasteful, yes, I know I'm hot and in control.

I've been wearing the same pair of trousers for a couple of months now, because I don't see any advantage in changing trousers. Because there isn't. I wash them and they dry overnight. She's twenty-six, twenty-seven? I would have still been fighting the garb wars at that age.

"Artemis, this is the nuts-and-bolts-and-chips ambassador of the man known as Bigger, because his bags are always going to be bigger than yours."

The robot shakes hands with Artemis. It's almost there. It's almost human movement. Give it a couple more years. A couple of tweaks. Faster chip. Bigger memory. I wonder why Bigger is so friendly to me because although we have some common ground in crypto, there are thousands of other afficionados in Dubai, and anyway you cut it, I barely rate as a patch of moss on his exceedingly long driveway.

But company is the most important thing. Whether it's friendship, or love, or just good company, that's what counts. If you're stranded in the jungle, or down a dungeon, or at a swanky party, or a big bed. Or a small bed. Company makes the difference. It doesn't get enough credit.

Did Bigger chose to be absent so he could play with his robot husk? It must have cost him a fortune. There can't be more than half-a-dozen robots knocking around the planet like this as we speak. How much does Bigger have?

We'll all have the robot extension soon. That's how tech leaps. My brother worked for a PR company. Gary got one of the first batch of Walkmans sent to Europe by Sony. One hundred, something like that. It was alien tech, fallen off the back of a flying saucer. Passers-by sank to their knees in awe. Traffic stopped. I'm not joking. I saw it. "It was like being David Bowie," Gary said. "I mean, when he was successful." It was a different era. Boom box. Walkman. Discman. iPod. iPhone. You don't even have to carry your music with you anymore. Once you had to manufacture your own music, blowing into a bone, rubbing things together like starting a fire. Now every layabout has a thousand orchestras and bands trailing behind.

Will kids be sending their bots to school? For thousands of years kids have trudged off to be bored, to wonder what geometry is good for, who cares about rainfall in Brazil, eat other people's lunches. Will they even send a bot? Will we need legs? They take up a lot of space. Ming said something about scientists in Shanghai trying to reduce all humans to three feet max, since it would make everything more manageable, save on resources. I couldn't tell whether he was joking. A robot ambassador is good for parties though, saves you the travel. Will we just live in pods with everything delivered?

"I like your art," Artemis says. "I used to work as muscle. I was the bodyguard for Holbein, Turner, Constable, Velázquez, all sorts of celebs." She did. She worked at the National Gallery. Escorted masterpieces round the world to other museums. Globe-trotted masterpieces. Stepped out with culture. I'm glad Not-Guilty isn't in earshot to learn of skinny chicks from soft schools toting fortunes around like a handbag.

"Celebs are hard work," Bigger agrees. "I always thought Velazquez was a twat. What do you do now?"

"I deal in passports," Artemis says. She does. There were characters in Catford who could get you fake passports, but you had to come recommended, some criminal record, and it cost a bomb. Her business is legit. All sorts of places, largely places you wouldn't want to live, will essentially flog you a passport, but it's legal, above board, and often doesn't cost a bomb.

Then there all sorts of loopholes people don't know about. If you have a grandparent with a certain nationality, you can claim your winnings. Artemis will save you the troublesome business of paperwork and knows the correct answers to the bizarre questions. Did you work in the nuclear industry in 1992?

Because if it's hard to make it, it's as hard to hold on to it. Legally or illegally. If she thinks she can sign up Bigger, I doubt he'll be interested. He'll probably have a smorgasbord of nationalities to escape to. But maybe not. Extreme wealth, you don't even need to bother with the paperwork. You can just have your superyacht or supersubmarine floating in international waters.

But you can't win. That's what I've learned. You can't win. You can only avoid losing for a long time. Enjoy it. They always come for you. Superyachts are easy to spot. In many ways being part of the crowd is good. Be ordinary. The best thing is to be like everyone else. Maybe with a bit more money than everyone else. Someone said so, somewhere, sometime.

Banks? They flop, go down. Property? Goes down. Gets burned down. Stocks? Companies go bankrupt. The folding stuff? Inflation. Taxes. Crypto? Exchanges go down. Wallets can be hacked. You can lose your seed phrase. Or you're encouraged to hand it over. Someone just holds a gun to your head or beats you with a chair leg.

NotGuilty was going on about how the old trick of sticking your wonga in your wife's name or best friend's care could go wrong. Never mind the tradition of good old-fashioned treachery. Your mate dies. Pegs out on the golf course. No one knows where he stashed the loot, because it was his job to hide it. So, he did. Your mate dies. Stung by a crazed Queen Bee. His Thai wife sells up, goes back to Thailand. If you make the mistake of going to Thailand to fuss, you'll be unhappy or dead.

I've spread it out. Stocks. Banks. Property. And the crypto. But I know I can't win. Nothing guarantees anything. Events. History. Things. Coming for you. Things. You can only stall. I missed the collapse of Mt Gox, the first great disaster in crypto, because I wasn't in crypto, I hadn't met Ming yet.

I missed the collapse of the biggest exchange, not because I was clever but because I had accounts at two other exchanges (spread it out, trust no one) and I couldn't be bothered to register for a third. It looked good, but I couldn't be arsed. Laziness was my pal. It saved me. Not foresight, good vision. A lot of wisdom-pushers went down with that moonship. It got crypto a bad name, although it had nothing to do with crypto. People. It was all to do with people. Never work with people. Including yourself. Someone will come along and mess it up. Rome. Babylon. Florence. Hiroshima. New York. San Francisco. Someone came along and messed it up.

I didn't get into Luna, because I was exhausted. Cream-crackered. Knackered. Keeping up with the news. Researching. Getting up early. Staying up late. Getting ready to duck as events take a swing. Researching convenient ways to commit suicide. Things. I had about twenty bags going by the time Luna took off and grizzled investors were getting Luna tattoos, and taking selfies of them, like teenagers in the throes of first love. I felt some regret when it was rocketing up, as you do when you see folk coining it. And I felt some relief when Luna crashed. But you can't do everything.

That's another lesson, you can't do everything. You can be ambitious, you should try a lot, no point aiming low. But you can't do everything. You can't catch every pump. Twenty bags, it's too much, unless you want to do nothing else with your life. No more than a dozen bags. Spread it around. Different chains. Defi. GameFi. AI. Because you never know. You never know when the palace will burn down. Take profits. You wake up and you've made thousands. That's a good feeling, and like a budding serial killer, you want more. That's it. It was like a licence to print money. I couldn't be arsed. I thought. No. No more. I really am too old for this. Let me just die next to the fireplace.

"You've got the best of nature, Bigger," I say nodding at Cedric, "and the best of tech.'

"And the best food," adds Math Cat, closing up his empty carton and wondering where to leave it.

"And the Art," says Artemis. Courtesy or cunning?

"Yeah, what about us, leave something for us," I say.

"Dan, have you been dabbling in the memes?" Bigger asks. "A taste of Pepe?'

It's a trick question. Like "Have you stopped beating your wife?" Degen action isn't for the old-timers. Hopping on and off fleeting tokens. The irony is that the bunch that made the towering fortunes, the dizzying amount of money, nation-slapping, face-melting money, weren't much concerned about the money. Satoshi walked away from billions. Leaving his wallet untouched. Or so it seems. It was the mission. They were missionaries.

"Pepe is on fire," says Math Cat. Some of the meme coins are more like nuclear explosions. Pepe didn't exist a month ago. Pepe is a cartoon frog, and not even what I'd call a well-drawn, or charming cartoon frog. And without any funny cartoon adventures. The gang behind Pepe took the trouble to say it has no value, to say it loudly, to say that they have no roadmap of development, that they have no connection with the guy who drew the shitty frog in the first place.

Pepe's a token running on Ethereum, with a website that features a cartoon frog. Setting up a token on Ethereum is now something anyone with a little bit of tech expertise can do in a few hours. Pepe is currently worth a billion dollars. A month ago, it didn't exist. In a few months it might be worth much less, but someone, somewhere has had their face melted.

There are fantastically intelligent people who spent years sweating, studying code. At hard-to-get-into universities. Who gave up weekends. Holidays. Who spent years working non-stop on complex crypto projects, with big teams, that will take years more to finalize. Who made themselves ill. Who spent years going to conferences drumming up attention. Whose project might do some good to others. They've been trampled by Pepe.

Trampled underfoot by a couple of semi-nerds who set up a token with an ugly cartoon frog they had nothing to do with, over a weekend, and who jived away with a fortune. You don't even have to be some full-time clued-up anorak to do that. Switching on a computer is enough.

Pepe. If you want hard evidence that it isn't fair, it isn't rational, and hard work doesn't work, stop here.

Crypto, it's the ultimate elevator. Create a token. Or jump on a token. Assistant masseurs at second division football clubs. Taxi drivers. Linen porters. Nail technicians. Dog groomers. Life coaches. They're all through the pearly gates, here in Dubai. It's brutal out there. So unfair. If you have talent or industry. Or fair. Why shouldn't the untalented or idle have a chance?

฿

Yes, there's a lot of unfairness knocking about. It was a lesson I learned early on.

I was on my own. My parents had gone shopping to have an argument about the purchase of a standing lamp. My brother, who usually spent Saturday in bed, had gone out to Old Compton Street. Gary liked to get some American wrestling magazines to show how jet-set he was and to jostle some arcade machines. Arcade machines, back then, short of armed robbery, were the pinnacle of bad-boy behaviour.

I had a date that evening, I was fifteen but nevertheless aiming for an unlimited flesh rampage and I was just about to leave. I was running late, but I was torn between two shirts, pondering about which shirt would be the better abetter. The blue or the red? The blue had the more up-to-date collar, but the red had a funky pattern. It was the age when you saw clothes as a weapon.

The doorbell rang. "Look sorry to bother you, my car's broken down," said the guy on the doorstep. "I tried the phone box on the corner, but it's out of order. Could I use your phone? Naturally, I'll pay.'" A phone call was an event then. An incident. Significant. It was a different era. My instinct was to close the door, but my mother had always urged us to be helpful to others, though it seemed idiotic to me, so I thought why not. He brandished a fifty pence piece, which was wildly generous for a quick call in those days.

As I hustled him out it occurred to me that he looked like David Bowie. But shorter. There were a lot of Bowie lookalikes drifting around then. He was South London's pride.

"You know, you really do look like David Bowie,' I said. He did, but shorter.

"That's probably because I am he. At your service." He did a theatrical bow. I only discovered later everyone in show biz is a midget. It's a midget conspiracy. "Do you want an autograph? Actually, I've got an album in the car if you want."

"Thanks. No."

I went with the blue shirt, because you've got to be up to date. I walked out of the house fast, but didn't run because I didn't want to sweat and waste the aftershave I'd splashed on. Bowie was waiting by his car as I sped by. I sang him a couple of lines that I suddenly remembered from "The Grinning Gnome" as I passed.

Then I concentrated on seeing if I could conjure up a combination of words that would cause female clothing to instantly fall to the ground.

It was only when I got on the bus to Beckenham for my date that... wait a minute. Wait a minute. I realised I should have got Bowie to sign the album for my brother. Bearing in mind Gary was a Bowie obsessive. Talked about very little else. I swear it just didn't occur to me.

Gary was always reading articles and books about Bowie, soaking up info. He had developed this theory. He was convinced, years earlier, we had unknowingly, accidentally seen Bowie getting married. We had gone shopping and as we walked past the Registry Office, there were all these weirdos. I remember that clearly, because hippies and weirdos were in short supply round our way then. It was a riot of weirdness. And that's where and roughly when Bowie did get married. Groups outside the Registry Office usually had ill-fitting suits they'd borrowed, looking awkward and unhappy. One of the well-weird weirdos must have noticed me goggle-eyed and said:

"Do you want an autograph?"

"No," I said. Because I was six and I had no idea what an autograph was.

"The circus must be in town," my father said. We laughed. My father explained what an autograph was on the bus home.

I had wanted Mr Phone User out of the house so I could go on my date. If someone had said to me in advance: Bowie will pop round on Saturday, I would have sorted it out, if nothing else just for the leverage. "Gary, remember the time I got you that signed Bowie album?" But my mind was on the date. You always arrive unprepared. The immediate unprepares you. I thought, well, I won't tell my brother. There was no Bowie, no phone call. I kept the fifty pence.

When I got back much, much, much later than was allowed,

they were all in the front room, waiting, like an interview panel. My brother was pale. Okay, I'm breaking the rules, give me the punishment, skip the lecture, please, but come on, no one died.

"What did Bowie have to say then?" asked my father.

The story was all over the street. After I left Bowie even did an à cappella version of "Space Whatever" for the gathering. It had been a fucking street party. Our across the street neighbour, Mrs Chester, who was a hundred, and always made you think about compulsory euthanasia, never left home, had no interest in music or anything apart from nosy-parkering, came out to talk about standing lamps with my parents and because she was always peering out, told them. Although Gary had already heard about the visitation from Tree-hugger Trev.

I thought about blanket denial. You always arrive unprepared. But it was so unlikely that Mrs Chester knew who Bowie was, it would be wrong to attempt there was no David Bowie. Or that it had been a Bowie imitator.

"Why didn't you get him to sign my albums?" my brother croaked.

"Of course, I asked. Why wouldn't I ask?" I said. Could I say he had a hand injury? I used that one later on in my career to delay signing a contract. You arrive unprepared. Given an hour's prep time I could have faked signatures or come up with a better yarn.

"He said he stopped signing things. He was a bit up himself, frankly. Rock stars." I shook my head. "And after I'd done him a favour."

"Trev from number eleven said he signed one," my brother exclaimed.

"Trev's making it up. You know what he's like," I countered, discovering like so many before me how lying is this vast slippery slope with obstacles popping up suddenly. How tiring it is. "Hey, I can sign the albums for you, everyone'll think it's genuine."

I was lucky though. My brother had it in for the Wheel rather than me. I was simply useless. Useless, in an incurable and predictable younger brother way. Destiny, Destiny however, had done him wrong. Mistreated him in a mean mistreating way. Mistreated by the Wheel. He hadn't been at home when Bowie rang the doorbell. He had put in the time. He had paid his dues. The hours, the days, the years, the decade he had spent at home scratching his scrotum, gazing at the ceiling, and no Bowie ringing the doorbell.

That was his takeaway, rather than his nitwit brother being too dozy ask for an autograph. I heard him sobbing that night. I honestly considered finding out where Bowie lived and begging for a signature to make amends. Or stealing one of his guitars. But it was a different era. It was difficult to find things out, so I didn't.

My father sat silent, not sure how to intervene on this one. That was the first time I managed to get something past him. Maybe.

฿

"Pepe? I stay away from cartoon frogs, cartoon frogs not my thing," I reply to Bigger. "I just sit on my bags these days. Like a fat, shagged-out dragon, shagged out on a pile of gold."

"Isn't that wrong," says Artemis. "A bit immoral? Didn't someone say you should use your money for good? A duty if you've made it"

"I'm sure someone, somewhere, sometime said so. I am using my bags for good. My good. If snoozing on my bags is immoral, it only makes it more enjoyable. And surely your job is all about giving your customers better tax deals and sunshine."

"And better odds of surviving a nuclear holocaust than the poor," Artemis replies. "Don't forget that. No one's wasting a nuke on Tonga."

"There you go. You titillate the rich. You collaborate with the rich. Or at least the not-poor. Isn't that failing on the morality front, basically a war crime?"

"But I'm a distressed arts graduate, who needs to earn a living."

"Yes," says Bigger. "Dan, you should make a splash every now and then. Make it rain in Spain, or make them prance in France, for instance." Bigger can do that. He can shift markets and probably does. Not that he tells anyone. No one knows about Bigger. Even if you do a search, you'll only find his real name on a few hits that give you no idea who he is or what he is. Complaints about planning applications in Swindon. A letter to Bowling News. Nothing about any company. Because he probably doesn't have any. He's a crypto native.

There is the Jesus Christ gig thing. You get rich, then you want to get loved. Generally, genuinely worshipped. Volunteer messiah. Buying love, not from an escort but from the public.

You won't find any profiles on him. He's not on any of the rich lists. I've had a fair amount to do with the press and I've learned that they're not very good. Lazy. Ignorant. To be fair, much like everyone else. No one wants to work. No one wants to think. All they do is copy each other's homework. Because they can. There are about two or three opinions on anything. Pick one. Pick a uniform. Pick an opinion. Then maybe for a bit of variety change sides late in your career.

I know one or two things. Not really secrets, because I know them. Not really secrets because there's no effort to conceal. What I've seen. What I've heard. Not really relevant to the course of events. Funny things. Surprising things. Things that journalists could have found out easily. If they'd looked in the right places. If they'd bothered looking. There's a pleasure in telling stories. There's also a pleasure in not telling stories, and sniggering.

How much does Bigger have? Quite a few early players had whopping sums of Bitcoin, but they lost it. Threw away the laptop. Or they sold up out of need, to buy a pizza, to buy a standing lamp, to buy a bike, a car, deposit on a house, even a house. To make it you had to hang on to it for years while your bag was laughed at as magic internet money, nerd badges, dumbo beans.

Diamond hands, or you forgot about it. Determination or laziness, they can both work. But if you had Bitcoin and you held it, you not only had the Bitcoin, you got the forks. You got the spin-offs. Bitcoin cash. Bitcoin gold. Etc. Free money. And Bigger would have got into Ethereum early on too.

It must have taken will-power to hang on.

I don't know why this never occurred to me before, but I think of something NotGuilty told me. We'd been chatting about crypto, something he dismissed as a joke, but he told me about a dealer he knew who had been found guilty and was about to be sentenced. He put all his cash into Bitcoin so the assets couldn't be seized or tracked, because then the law knew as much about crypto as the Jakarta bus timetable on a Sunday. The dealer then packed his toothbrush and dressing gown ready for jail.

"Why didn't he do a bunk?" I asked.

"You or I might do that, Dan, because that would be the intelligent move. Scarper off to Turkey for a few years. Eat those kebabs. Lie on some historic beaches. Jet ski in some historic water. Come back home, no one will be looking for you. But some people can't leave Catford. It's too much. Too much for the nut. And for some people, not everyone, but some people jail is like a hotel. Maybe not a good hotel, with wonky room-service, but you're not paying, are you? And it's a members' club, where you can network, but you pay no annual fee. He does his three years, gets out, Bitcoin has rocketed, and he buys a mansion in the countryside with the profits. Although he hardly ever goes there, because it's too far from Catford."

Bigger in jail? I wonder if Bigger had been in jail so he couldn't spend it? That thought had never occurred to me before. What if Satoshi didn't walk away selflessly from crypto? What if he's doing life somewhere for bumming and killing kids, unable to get at his wallet? What if he really did have a boating accident?

If his laptop is at the bottom of a lake? I don't care. My bags are big. I've straddled the world, even if the world didn't notice. I've nattered with royalty and paupers, the famous and the hidden, like Bigger.

I take what tastes like an egg soufflé with chutney from a server. Always eat the canapés.

"I almost forgot." Bigger turning towards me. "Happy birthday, Dan." Okay this interest in me is now getting odd. Also, some people have the gab to pull off manipulation. Bigger might have been standing in the right place when the Bitcoin flowed like water, but he's not in the running as a con man. His 'almost forgot' falls like a dumbbell to the floor, He's been waiting all evening for that.

"Well, Happy Birthday us, I should say."

"You too? What today?"

"Nothing like being a Gemini." Math Cat, Artemis, Hamad, the token Emirati Bigger has generously invited, two Dutch hydrologists and a Swiss senior locust forecaster who've joined us, do a rousing version of "Happy Birthday". The hydrologists make a hydrology joke. There wasn't a locust joke.

Whenever I hear Gemini I think of my Big Cousin, whose birthday was the same day as mine. He was five years older, but the family had a lot of joint birthday parties to save money. Maybe that was why we were close. But alarm bells are ringing now, because it's also a classic bonder. "Oh, you have the same birthday as me. We're special."

Bigger's now done the groundwork. Is he going to ask for a loan? Or what?

Bigger's robot reaches to Artemis's ear. "You're growing coins," he pulls out a coin. It's that basic magic trick of pulling out a coin to dazzle kids. It's odd how ancient, how Victorian, a coin looks. It looks like it should be in a museum. I imagine the coin has been carefully selected for prestidigitation. The robot hand pulls the coin out, but then muffs it at the last stage and the coin rolls away on the floor. Almost. Almost there.

I offer to escort Artemis home. As we leave, I see NotGuilty chatting with the two Dutch hydrologists. They're quite attractive, but he's not on the pull. NotGuilty's had his cage rattled by something. Really rattled. I hope he won't cause a scene. He's a few pounds overweight and no one our age is fast, but he has arms that have seen a lot of weights. And I've watched him punch the bag in the gym. Those are powerful muscles, and he punches smooth. Those arms were made for fighting. He hits you a bone is breaking. Jaw. Rib.

"Quick word, Dan," NotGuilty says conspiratorially. An angry conspiracy. "That thing."

"Thing?"

"The thing I left with you. I'll come over later on and pick it up, if it's okay with you." NotGuilty fails badly on the okay-with-you bit.

Perhaps it's growing up in Catford, but I nearly always mull over what I'd do in a fight with someone. With NotGuilty my only hope would be to go first, with a weapon, a chair, golfclub, a frying pan, something heavy that would keep me out of his reach. There was a guy in Catford who had a frying pan sown onto the back of his coat. This was just after punk when all sorts of bollocks was being glued or sown onto clothes. He would rip off the frying pan when things got heated and apparently was very handy with it. I suppose he practiced.

"Thanks for the invitation, that's one of the most interesting evenings I've ever had," Artemis says. "Did you talk to that American guy, who works at NASA, Jamie?"

"No."

"He's in the search for non-human intelligence. Alien hunter. I asked him if he'd been to Area 51. He said, 'we don't keep them there anymore.'"

"So where do they keep them?'

"I might have found out if I'd slept with him. He looked like he hadn't been out for a gallop lately. But I don't care that much. If they're here, they're here. They might have been at the party."

"I didn't see any green men."

"You see you're making assumptions. What if they're exactly like us, warts and all? And they've made deals with the government?"

"No advanced intelligence would make a deal with a government. They'd want to talk to some adults."

Later on, I drive out to Ming's to collect the pink boulder. I guess in a few days I'll be driving back to return it.

฿

I have seen perfect, not-a-shadow-of-a-doubt, total happiness. At least once. When we were on holiday in Torquay, my son who was four, ran ahead of us into a café, then ran out, yelling: "They have ice cream."

฿

Bitcoin is at thirty thousand. Has been for a while. Flat as a pancake. No one knows what to say. Even revolutions have their boring bits.

At her request, I have lunch with Artemis. She's considering investing in crypto. She chooses her meal much faster than her mother.

"There's just so much going on. Just so much information about crypto," she says. "It's like a party with too loud music and everyone off their tits on crazy drugs, grabbing you."

"I'm not going to argue."

In a way I've stopped in crypto. I have a few familiar bags, and I don't pay much attention to the new stuff. I stay at home, as it were. I'm a crypto shut-in. Because it's growing so fast in so many directions and is so complicated, it's exhausting. It's too much. Like quantum mechanics. What's it like to be the same age as Artemis now? Isn't it all too much?

My parents, that generation, the Second World War batch, were physically rationed. Little to eat. My generation had some rationing. We had some limits. We didn't have unlimited television. We didn't have unlimited music. We didn't have unlimited films. We didn't have unlimited news. We certainly didn't have unlimited porn. I would have walked ten miles, over broken glass, to see a pair of naked breasts when I was thirteen. It was a different era. Travel abroad to America, to Japan, even some of Europe was cripplingly costly. Rock star stuff. You did join the army to see the world. We didn't have unlimited knowledge, or so much knowledge that for us mortals it might as well be unlimited, by prodding a computer. Want to learn Basque? Want to build a nuke? It's at your fingertips. When you have it all, where do you start? And where do you stop?

"The crypto channels are chuckling," she says.

"Yes, they are," I reply.

The American authorities, slowly, clumsily, like all authorities have been straining to clamp down on crypto. Everyone pays attention to the Americans. No one cares about the Brits or the Swiss. The Americans have just lost a major court case against crypto and their dignity. The price of crypto should be rocketing moonward, but it isn't.

"I saw Math Cat," Artemis says. "I asked him whether this was a good time to invest. I didn't get a yes. Or a no."

"No, he doesn't do that."

"He said you need to start looking at the 1940s and income tax rates. Was he joking?"

"No."

What I enjoy about moments like this is that it demonstrates, finally, that no one knows anything. Nothing guarantees anything. Math Cat could explain this recent flatness in Bitcoin all afternoon. It's easy to come up with explanations for the past. Or even the just departed present. The future's not such a pushover.

"Have you met Magenta? His girlfriend?"

"Don't ask me to explain. No one can. Although I did have a flatmate once who was a hypnotist. He had a girlfriend, let's say more beautiful than you'd expect."

"What do you think about the market?"

"I'd say the boom time is over. Silly gains are gone. Your face isn't in danger of being melted. Bitcoin's another asset. Commodity. A Picasso. Thing. We're basically the stock market, but not everyone has realized that. You're three years too late. Golfclubs in the Jurassic."

"Golfclubs in the Jurassic?"

"Wrong thing, wrong time."

"Any tips on how to get to the right place. At the right time? With the right thing?"

I thought about that one. "No."

"That's a lifetime's worth of experience?"

"Yes."

"So, you're saying the simplest solution would be to build a time machine, go back twelve years and buy some baby Bitcoin."

"Maybe. But no more than maybe. Nothing guarantees anything."

"What, history doesn't teach us anything? The past is useless? Should be thrown out with the rubbish?"

"Some say history repeats. Some say history rhymes. I say both are true. I can predict the future accurately, with a hundred per cent reliability. It will rain. It will snow. There will be an earthquake. Someone will start a war. Someone will run off with a large sum of money. Someone will say why didn't someone stop that? History does repeat, but when? This afternoon at ten past three? Next Thursday?"

I felt as someone who'd been around, I should offer more. "You can't create opportunities. You can only ride them. That's why you have to pay attention. Attentive ignorance."

It's embarrassing that crypto is now largely in step with the stock market. The stock market. That moss-covered thing they've had for hundreds of years. Like steam engines. Stock market goes up, crypto goes up. Stock market goes down, crypto goes down. Stock market stagnant, crypto stagnant. With a touch of irregularity, so Math Cat can make a living.

"But doesn't Bitcoin change everything? Help the unbanked? Isn't that the slogan?"

I'm a crypto lifer, but the messianic ejaculations? Come on.

"No one helps the unbanked. You need to be careful where you're born. The boon to humanity argument is daft. Bitcoin has helped a few humans, not humanity. But they could have got ahead by betting on the gee-gees, or camels or stocks. Bitcoin is a new convenience." That's rather good, I think. I should make a note of that.

"Is it true they have robot jockeys for their camel races here?"

"They're not robot jockeys, they're remote-controlled whips. Furthermore," I add, deeming myself aged and wise, "No one really helps anyone."

"That's not true, Dan. You're overboard."

"You'll see. Cancer. Ageing. Death. You're a spectator. You can wring your hands, love as much as you want, but you stay a by-stander."

"But the tech – "

"Never mention the tech to anyone in crypto. They'll laugh at you."

"What about the aesthetics then? What about the aesthetics of Bitcoin?" Artemis says. Is she aware I poked her mother so hard she came six times? She didn't know which planet she was on. Do mothers and daughters go there? Does she care?

"Anyone who talks about the aesthetics of Bitcoin, is an aesthetic-nutter who needs to talk about aesthetics. Usually with too much time on their hands. Ideas and people don't mix well. The problem with crypto is not crypto, it's people. You can have a great idea, sooner or later, a person will come along and mess it up."

I'm here for the loot and the laughs. It's fun to throw a brick through a window. Revolutions don't turn the world upside down. However it looks. They change things a little. For teenage crypto, it's like rushing to a party and finding your grandfather there in his pyjamas. You check the address, and yes, you're at the right place, but it's not what you expected.

"What about spirituality?" Artemis asks. She's winding me up now.

"Be spiritual when you're dead."

"That's a sweeping statement, Dan. You need an orange juice to sweeten you up."

"I'd love to be around to talk to you when you're in your sixties. Maybe you'll be sweeter than me. Crypto's here to stay. But nothing really changes. Eggs. Don't put them all in the same basket. There's a reason you hear that. Again, and again. Put some in one basket. But have other baskets. Spread your dough around."

"Hey, we do help each other. You're helping me now with your crypto wisdom. Maybe not as often as we should. But we do help each other."

"If you can't raise the dead, you can't truly help anyone." I paused. "If you can't raise the dead, you're a timewaster." I've no idea where that came from. It was like someone else speaking. Like I was a ventriloquist's dummy.

"What about the Big Bastard? What's going on there?" Artemis asks.

"Mr Wall Street himself? Cut him and he bleeds billions?"

The crypto channels are also ablaze with equally big news. The Biggest Bastard of the biggest asset management firm in the world. Pharmaceutical-strength finance. The Supreme Being, the highest of the high, has given the thumbs-up to Bitcoin.

"Is the fortress waving the white flag?"

It's not a fake video. No one has kidnapped his kids. There is no gun to his head. According to him, not only is Bitcoin okay, it's as good as those famous slips of paper, the dollar or the euro. Indeed, wait for it, it's probably better. Better. That's what he said. And he's shouting this from the clock tower. Why isn't the price of Bitcoin out of control? Nothing guarantees anything, and the blessing had been coming, spotted way down the road. It's amusing because three years ago, he and his chums were hawking up big ones and gobbing on Bitcoin.

"They're waving a flag," I say. "Whatever they're saying, whatever they're doing, it's not for our benefit."

"But crypto's won," Artemis insists. "They have bowed down to the majesty of Bitcoin." She raises her glass. I raise mine.

So, we've won. Evidence says so. The American government slapped around in court, and the well-hung financiers unzipping and getting ready to mount up. I've learned to be wary about winning. I thought I'd won a couple of times. So be careful. In any case, I'm not bothered that much about Bitcoin's trajectory.

One way or another, I won't be around much longer. When you're over sixty, every time you purchase a mattress, a lamp, a computer, you can't help thinking this might last longer than me. I'm not going to have marvellous adventures now, or set myself up as a warlord in a failed state, because, if for no other reason, I like an afternoon kip.

฿

Back then, I thought I'd won when Vikki phoned.

"I'm coming back to London," she said. "I've had enough of LA. The mess that never ends."

I had won. Smacked the world in the mouth. Beaten the Wheel. After Vikki's announcement, I walked through Hyde Park. The sun was shining. A perfect temperature. I had a job I liked. Some major plans planned. The only good in the world, was finally returning to me. I was going to get her pregnant. What more was there? Sorted. I'd won.

I'd never had such a sensation of victory. There was an Italian woman with outrageous tits, sunbathing by the Serpentine. Oiling her breasts in a severely oiling her breasts way that shouldn't be allowed. Very unfair. I didn't care. I was out of the game. I walked with a swagger, but a restrained swagger, because if you've won, there's no need to show off. No need for exertion. I congratulated myself. You're on top, Dan. I knew you had it in you.

All the effort had been worthwhile. All the excuses I had made to do business in LA. All the flights. I'd been living on planes. It had been a slog. Our time together in LA was fairly strained, because Vikki was so knotted up. So contorted with the divorce.

I had to listen to non-stop moaning about the Livermore Lab. Livermore is the Wimbledon of nuking. Or so Vikki said. Vikki had always been convinced that somehow she could get her foot in the door. Particularly from LA. It's true the Livermore is in California, but San Francisco's a long walk from LA.

On the other hand, she lived across the road from Caltech. I knew, I still know, nothing about quantum and confinement physics, but Caltech is littered with Nobel winners, apparently a good sign. When I first discovered Caltech was across the road from her, an easy-to-cross road, a two-minute walk, I suggested why not go over and say hello? Volunteer. Hang out. Buy someone a drink. Join their badminton society. What have you got to lose? If you can't get to the Wimbledon of nuking, how about the Roland Garros? If Roland Garros is just across the road?

No one listens to me much, I've noticed. Vikki was obsessed with the Livermore, and once obsession sets up camp, a cup of tea and a chat won't change anything.

"They don't reply to my letters. It's so unprofessional." Vikki would curse the Livermore as I thought: you're now so batshit crazy, divorce-doolally, dear, I wouldn't trust you with a broom, let alone anything nuclear. She was in a very unhappy situation, seriously alone, in a rough city, no driving licence, but she wasn't good company. She had one former colleague from home living in LA, but I wasn't surprised once she said, "Sasha doesn't return my calls."

I admired her grit. But if you want to win a fight, choose a fight you can win. Someone said so, somewhere, sometime. I had to listen to round-the-clock moaning about judges, lawyers, dog-walkers, leaf-blowers. How she had to change lawyers and therapists like laundry. Fresh lawyers, fresh therapists, fresh drugs. Fresh dog-walkers. Like a drunk at throwing-out time, she would get into wasteful rows to add to the load.

"Why not quit the antidepressants?"

"I have to be on antidepressants, otherwise how can I prove to the judge I'm depressed?" Vikki said.

"Just walk away," I said. "You're better off just walking away."

I was so exposed to all the intricacies, the ups and downs, well, mostly the downs, it was like getting divorced myself. But I knew some faces in LA. Some old ones.

I was in a bodega late one night, when the guy in front of me was having trouble paying for some chewing gum and some chocolate biscuits. His credit card wasn't working and he didn't have enough cash. It was David Bowie.

"South London solidarity," I said. "Let me take care of that."

He was very grateful. Offered to take my details. Have his entourage drop the dollars off.

"No. No. My pleasure," I said.

"Would you like an autograph?"

"No," I said. Gary had got an album signed somehow. He had it framed on a wall. We laughed about that. Gary had also gone off Bowie a bit because of that Bin Machine business.

I'd won. Vikki was coming back. Walking away from the legal quagmire in LA. Coming back to me.

I don't know why the divorce degenerated so badly. Jasper wasn't a shitty vicious guy. Just human. He liked having things his own way, and he found it difficult to stop actresses sitting on his face. But he was a film director, so he was used to endurance. Trained. To the marathon. To not giving in. He was pushing his film about Scott of the Antarctic, which didn't feature the Antarctic, but was set in a small room in Dumfries.

Vikki didn't hate him. Angry. Disappointed. Most champions have the desire to win, to crush opponents. But there is a category of players who thrive to some extent because they can't bear losing. They hate losing and will fight relentlessly, more for that than to win. Jasper and Vikki didn't have a lot of money, and nearly all of that went to the lawyers. For Vikki it wasn't about winning because does half a garden hose matter? It was more about refusing to lose.

And Vikki did fly back to London.

I had won. For half-a-day. I had wanted to be at the airport to meet her, but I couldn't as I had to be in France for business. She phoned me from Heathrow airport. "I wanted to say that I'm getting back on a plane to LA," she said. "Sorry."

I tried rational arguments again. Obviously, they didn't work.

Then I had moaning about the suitcase she'd bought to come back to London. She'd discovered it was sold for twenty dollars less in another shop. She didn't think, well, I should have shopped around harder.

This was a crime. A major crime. Vikki had been swindled. Targeted. She took the suitcase back to try to reclaim her twenty dollars. It became as important as the divorce. She had lost the receipt, and by now it was a used suitcase, so even the most extravagant customer service wouldn't have yielded. Misery and rage had gobbled up her sense of perspective. There does come a point, either physically or mentally, when you can't look after yourself. And if you don't have family or friends around you . . .

That was the moment I decided I had to do something. Was I going to sit around and hope? Or was I going to take charge? Are you a man or a small mammal waiting for some flying lobster?

It was a slow process. One Sunday morning lying in bed, I was wondering whether I had the bottle, the brass neck, to pull the trigger and shoot Jasper. Take the weight. Not everyone can. My Big Cousin told me stories of punters coming into Catford nick, thirty years after topping someone, to confess, to puke it all up. They couldn't take the weight. I imagined shooting Jasper. I imagined apologizing to him first. Nothing personal.

Then, to my surprise, Jasper called. I hadn't talked to him for a while.

"Dan, big hello from LA. Is it raining? I'm not disturbing you, am I?'

"Not at all. How's Hollywood?"

"Terrible. Terrible. You could spend your entire life here doing meetings. A million meetings, a million meetings to extract one maybe, maybe. But I'm working on a project about Scott of the Antarctic. Very hopeful. Very hopeful about that."

"Don't forget to pack your thermal undies."

"We won't be shooting in the Antarctic. Look, I know you're a busy beaver, and I hope you don't think my calling is too odd. Have you heard about Vikki and me? We're divorcing."

Have I heard? I'd heard almost nothing else.

"Yes. Sorry to hear about that." I wasn't lying. I was sorry to hear another fucking word on the subject.

"It's turning into a bit of a saga, I'm afraid. Never talk to a lawyer if you can avoid it. Avoid them like the plague. I know you were pally with Vikki, going to all those piano recitals. Vikki always spoke highly of you." I doubt that. If I have a poker face, she had sealed lips. Need to know. She would have made a great spy. Almost a black hole, information went in, almost nothing came out.

"I hope you don't mind me asking for your help. It would be better for her to go home. It would be better for me to go home, but I'm stuck here. I've tried to talk it out, but we're too deep in our trenches. The whole thing is ridiculous. I know it's a horrendous imposition. We need a diplomat. A peacemaker. We need a reason-bringer. Someone to put in a word for good old reason. That sort of thing. Would you be willing talk to her?"

"What's her number?" Notice, I didn't say I didn't have it. Did Jasper know how pally we were? Women always know. They may not know how, where, when, who. But they know. They're bizarrely sensitive on that. Men often don't. Maybe women are better actresses. Maybe smarter.

But even if Jasper didn't know about us, he was calling in cock. A delivery of dick. He was inviting me to do his wife. To cart her off. Either some sweettalking or a hard pounding. Take her off my hands. Please. I admired the front. I admired the ruthlessness. Whatever it takes. Total-war Jasper. Mate, I'm giving it to your wife as hard as I can, I promise you, but she just won't budge.

That's when I decided Jasper had to go.

Not long after, I was in St Petersburg on business, and one evening I went into a restaurant. Where I saw Vikki.

Vikki was sitting at a table with three others. I couldn't believe it. How? What's the strangest thing that could happen to you in this restaurant? Absolutely the last thing I could have expected. I had a mixture of anger and pleasure. I stared for a bit. It was definitely her. What was she doing here? She was supposed to be in Los Angeles, locked in limitless litigation. Was it some practical joke?

I walked up to her table and she glanced at me and returned to the conversation. "Hello," I said. She said something in Russian. The complete lack of recognition, the puzzlement in her eyes made me realize it couldn't be Vikki.

But I want to make it clear, she didn't look a lot like Vikki. She was identical. There was a hint of a crease then in Vikki's forehead, that was there. She even dressed like Vikki and smirked at me like Vikki. It was spooky. Frightening. It was the most unnerving experience I've ever had, outside of a dream. Like being in an accident. I had to leave the restaurant, it was so unsettling. And they did terrific Siberian dumplings in that place. I did check with Vikki whether she had some lost twin somewhere.

That's just to say, no matter how odd you think you are, how unlike everyone else, you are part of a batch. I once saw a Japanese porn film. I assume it was meant to be a porn film, but you never know with the Japs. It had two hundred couples in a warehouse, at it. I suppose the theory was one couple good, two couples better, etc. Pile it on.

You had these two hundred couples in synchronized grappling, going through the same movements at the same time. It was fresh, but it wasn't exciting, there was something about it that made me sad. Most of us would put the moments in someone else's arms as the best, or one of the best moments. But the act that was so precious, so unique, so redeeming, choose your own adjective here, whatever, the same thing was going on to the left, the right of you, in front and behind. How ordinary even the highlights are . . .

It's the bickering that glues you together, as much as any lust. My father always went on about my nails not being clean enough, even the week before he died. My wife would tell me I couldn't lace up my trainers properly. It was annoying because she was right.

It took me a long time to realize that if you don't have pestering like this, you're unlucky.

฿

Leaving my flat, I bump into NotGuilty leaving his. Was he lurking? "Dan. Mate. Come on in. You've got to have a birthday drink with me."

He's got a pinball machine and a jukebox in his flat. I've never managed to put the 1970s behind me. I admit I rebought some of my favourite comics a while ago, to relive those pleasures. Fractionally. But NotGuilty's really stuck. The pinball machine and the jukebox are beautifully redone. Money and time was spent. They probably weren't that spick and span when they first left the factory.

I have no desire to play pinball again. None. It was a different era. It was one of those things you did in the 1970s because there was nothing much else to do. And if you made a lot of noise, you might attract some female attention. I played some of my son's video games, the ones where you keep shooting people, and that was fun for half-an-hour, and much better than pinball.

Jukeboxes were a novelty for a party until, oh, just after the millennium. But now your phone has thousands more songs, in less scratchy quality.

"Get that down your laughing hatch." NotGuilty hands me a glass of champagne. He has a slug, then lets out a sigh of satisfaction. "That's quite a champagne." I was worried he might call it unapologetic.

"Monstro. Monstro champagne," I say to show approval. I don't want to tell NotGuilty I couldn't care less about champagne. I say 'monstro' occasionally, even though it sounds stupid. My Big Cousin used to say that, although he knew it sounded stupid. That was the joke. I say it as a tribute, as commemoration. I use flibbertigibbet from time to time because it was my mother's choicest term of condemnation. Only my brother can pick up on that.

The exuberance stops. As if a brake has been applied. NotGuilty can change mood like a teenager. A moody one.

"Champagne," NotGuilty continues. "Champagne. That was my weirdest court case. Some bloke drowned in his jacuzzi. Why they thought it was anything to do with me? Not going to lie, that was quite stressful that one. Went on for a long time. Don't recommend going on trial for murder. Although the Old Bailey's a fantastic building. Definitely a court to visit. The history. What's that word they use? Redolent. Redolent of history. Pongs of history. You're part of history there. You ever been accused of murder?"

"No."

"Ever murdered anyone, Dan?"

"No."

"You must have thought about doing it?"

"No."

"You liar."

I'm old. I'm wily. Am I still arriving unprepared for some things? Obviously. But attentive ignorance can pay off. In small ways. I've learned no giveaways. Not to someone like NotGuilty. It's rarely idle banter with him. He's sharp. But it's a common failing with the clever, they often don't take into account that they're not the only brain in the room.

It wasn't a snap decision to bump off Jasper one afternoon. I had nothing against him personally.

But if you have everything in front of you. Everything you could ever want. As far as you're concerned, everything. The best of the world, wrapped up in one person. Could you be wrong? Perhaps. But you don't feel that. You feel you're right. You have everything just in front of you. Just a little way out of your grasp.

The prize. You can clearly see it. Everything. No doubt. It's all there. You have nothing behind you. Nothing. And someone is standing between you and everything. Are you just going to dawdle there?

Shooting Jasper was a joke at first. But as the divorce proceedings rolled on, the humour faded. The notion of pulling a trigger crept up slowly, like a flu. Would I have gone through with it, face to face, in the end? I don't know. You don't know how you'll behave in extreme circumstances, until the extreme circumstances arrive. Handing over the match. When my mother died, I didn't cry. I'd always imagined I'd go to pieces when she died, and eventually I did, but I didn't cry.

It was a different era. I couldn't do it now. In fact, now, it's impossible to get away with a crime in most places. Forensics, cameras, phones, all that. If they're willing to throw the kitchen sink into it, they'll find you. If you walk past a greengrocer's now, you'll leave an autograph on an avocado. Your only hope is that they don't reach for the kitchen sink. It's not like the 1970s where the police would make lame appeals for info from the public, precisely because they had sod all. It's a little frightening in a way, that a freedom has been taken away.

Travel into the US, from Mexico. That was my plan. Not a false passport, a genuine one, just not mine. This was the era when no one looked like their passport photo and no one cared. Make my way to LA. Stay with a friend, who wasn't a gun nut, but close. Almost every drawer in the house had a gun. Borrow a Glock (I'd been on ranges). Find Jasper alone. Shoot him. Change barrel in gun, so no blowback on friend. Leave country.

I didn't say a word to Vikki. Maybe she would have objected. Although at that stage I doubt it. Not because I didn't trust her, but because there was no need. With the fury of their divorce so expensively, so extensively recorded, the law would be onto her like a ton of bricks. She wouldn't have to lie when they came to question her. They couldn't break her because there was nothing to break.

One afternoon, my Big Cousin said to me, out of the blue: "Listen, you tosspot. You're not the type. But if you ever do anything heavy, okay? Don't tell anyone. No one. Not me. Not your girlfriend. Not some stranger on a train. Not a priest. If you can't keep your mouth shut, you can't expect anyone else to, can you? You know how the police, nine times out of ten, find out? Someone told someone. If no one knows, no one knows."

He added some advice about shoes. "If you do do something, get a pair of shoes one size too big."

฿

"You never ever thought about killing someone?" NotGuilty has a second go. Are we wired for sound?

"Some road-rage moments."

"We've all had those. Yeah, no fun, up on a murder charge. Even if you get a good seat at the Old Bailey. Don't recommend it at all."

"What did the champagne have to do with it? Sloshed, was he?"

"You could say that. He drowned in vintage champagne."

"Must have been a lot of champagne."

"Only about three inches or so. It was his collection of vintage champagne. From la-de-dah auctions. Poetic, isn't it? Drowning in your collection of classy champagne. Is that the word. No, ironic. Iconic? The wrath of grapes. That's a film, isn't it?'

"Difficult to drown in three inches."

"You know how many drownings there are in bathtubs? You'd be surprised how many drownings happen in bathtubs. If you're drunk. On meds, or have some fit. Even if you're sober as a judge. My brief said that with a big smile. Even if you're sober as a judge, you can slip, bang your head. Down you go. That's that.

"My brief had piles of stats about drowning. How unlucky you can be with booze. The prosecution argued that this flash fucker wasn't an unlucky drunk. But your home is more dangerous than sharks, that's a fact. Homes are serial killers. No, the prosecution argued that he wasn't drunk, but someone who'd allegedly cheated all his associates, and had been drowned that way. As a message. But I wouldn't know anything about that. That's why they found me not guilty. Ever been cheated, Dan? Short-changed. Swindled?"

"Does a bear shit in the woods?"

"Yeah. Revenge. Revenge is a funny old business."

Revenge. So much has been said about that. Someone said so, somewhere sometime. It's this and that. Not much agreement on this one.

"Revenge. It never quite works out," NotGuilty continues. "One bloke I knew, Lenny. Heavy-duty type. Got shafted by someone. Can't remember what it was about. Money, most likely. Lenny spent ten years looking for him, finally found him. Got the debtor trussed up, gagged, you know in some disused garage so the mess wouldn't matter. Gave him the big speech about how furious he was. Jumping up and down. "You think you can do that to me? To me?" Explained that he was going to kick him to death. Lenny'd brought his heavy-duty boots. Frothing at the mouth so much, he could barely do them up. Gave the debtor one kick, not a good one, without a big run up. Just the one tap, and then Lenny collapsed. Heart attack. Dead. He'd done a lot of coke over the years, bad for your old cardio-vascular. The guy who was supposed to be the casualty eventually managed to worm his way out of the ropes, went home with a small bruise."

"Revenge, yes, it's tricky, too much like hard work," I agree.

NotGuilty is unaware that he's only alive and sipping champagne because of a distant Russian missile taking out a flying Serbian hitman with a full orderbook. Boban-the-Blown-Up-Butcher had plans for him. But you never know. Maybe Boban-the-Blown-Up-Butcher would have blown it. Even the no. 1 seed stumbles. My guess is there must have been a number of attempts to do final harm to NotGuilty.

I was unaware too that NotGuilty was Boban's project, until this morning when Trev confirmed to me that his cheating, career-destroying partner was none other than NotGuilty. Something stirring in the back of my mind finally prompted me to ask that question, to wonder whether two and two should be put together.

Why had NotGuilty got involved with an unsuccessful bike shop and lentil promotion business? It was so unlikely that it had taken me quite a while to work round to that possibility. Money laundering? Or just the prospect of easy, if small pickings? Did he just turn Trev over because he could? Because Trev was there? Trev wasn't a close friend, but it was hard not to feel that I had some duty, some requirement to make some gesture to settle up scores. Trev had only made the mistake of living decently. Fine, NotGuilty had saved my life, but he'd only been walking down some stairs.

Depriving NotGuilty of his toy, his bauble, not his life would be a fitting punishment. Although his rage at losing his pink boulder might well kill him. But how? How can I arrange that without any inconvenience to me? Pretend there was a burglary? NotGuilty certainly believes someone's looking for it. But our building is covered with cameras, although of course no one noticed me puking my life out on the stairs. Revenge is hard work. I'll have a think. Maybe inspiration will come during my afternoon kip.

"You still want me to look after the doorstop?" I ask. "I almost broke my toe on it this morning."

"If you don't mind. It's an interesting object. My mate Harvey who knows people who know people, who know other people, he was told that the gang that did the Brink's Mat robbery didn't know the gold would be there."

"You've mentioned that." At least a dozen times.

"That gold. It was like a bonus. And as they were leaving, one of the gang saw a box, also outside the vault. As a lucky dip, he picked it up, threw it on top. That doorstop, as you call it, was in the box."

"What does your mate Harvey say it is?"

"It's interesting, for a start. Because it doesn't exist."

"My toe would argue it does."

"You know how much ruction there was about that robbery? How many newspaper articles, how many books? How many court cases? Insurance investigations? Endless fuss about what colour underwear the guards were wearing that day? Every detail examined. Re-examined. Debated. One thing, one thing was never mentioned anywhere, ever. Not once. That doorstop, it's like it was never at Brink's-Mat.'

"Maybe it wasn't. Harvey could be wrong. Maybe he misunderstood something."

NotGuilty doesn't like that. I've crossed a line.

"I have a lot of faith in Harvey. Back in dear old Catford, when I was a kid. I had a good friend, Bazza. For some reason, our names got mentioned in relation to an armed robbery. That's how gossip is. It was my first court case. Bazza got windy, took a train to Glasgow, spent eight hours hiding in the toilet because he had no ticket. I wanted to clear my name, I went to court, where I was found not guilty. Meanwhile, up in Jockland, Bazza had signed up for the army. He loved it. Absolutely loved it. Couldn't get enough. Eventually, he joined them."

"Them?"

"Yeah, them."

"Sorry, who's them?"

"You know. The Hereford Gun Club. Them. Every now and

then, we'd meet up. Bazza had lots of funny stories. About things they did to the Russians. And the Americans. You got to tell someone, haven't you? No matter how secret your job is, you've got to spill sometimes. I won't tell you his stories because I promised him to keep my mouth shut. They are truly hilarious. There's one about a jar of piss. You wouldn't believe it. But not long after the Brink's Mat, we met and he told me they had been tasked to find the contents of that box. Thought I might know something."

"Did you mention Harvey?"

"It wasn't right to drag Harvey into it."

"Did he say what it was? Is it some weird artwork?"

"They hadn't been told what it was. Need-to-know crap. Bottom line: get the fucking thing back. The problem with using someone who is especially good at finding out things, is that he's good at finding out things."

"What did he reckon?"

NotGuilty looks at me. Thinking it over.

"He said. And I quote. It's a starship engine."

I laugh. I can't stop laughing. Then I notice NotGuilty, very angry. He's probably one of those types who think any laughter in the vicinity might be directed in some way at him. This time it is.

"Come on. Don't take the piss."

"I'm not taking the piss." NotGuilty is seething.

"I don't know what it's meant to be, but it's just some rock."

"You know, do you? What a fucking starship engine looks like?"

That's true. I'm not an interstellar engineer.

"It fell off the back of a starship, did it?"

"It was recovered from a crash site." The hostility, seeping out of NotGuilty, dripping onto the floor, is worrying me. I'm too old for a fight. Even with someone as old as me. I look around for a weapon. If he snaps, I'll have to glass him with the champagne flute. That's sophistication.

"Look, let's say it is," I offer submission. "My question to you is this: Why do you want it? What good is it? You can't build a starship around it."

"Insurance. It's good to have insurance." I've heard that. In the world of crime, sometimes you steal things so you can hand them back later, for a reduction. Often something you can't fence. Priceless art works.

"You tell no one about it." NotGuilty goes for the unveiled threat as I leave. If you can't keep your mouth shut, is it my fault?

"Believe me, I'm not telling anyone."

I'll say this for Dubai. You can have just about anything delivered to your door in an hour. I drive over to Ming's with the Geiger counter and give the pink boulder a once over while Ming consults the manual. "You're beginning to worry me Dan."

The needle didn't shift.

₿

A week later, I heard voices, movement, outside my flat. I opened my door and they're wheeling a body out of NotGuilty's flat. Zipped up in a bag, with no need for oxygen. It has to be NotGuilty. To be honest, I feel relief. I get some peace. Ming gets a garden ornament.

Cornelia is watching. Her face confirms the bad news.

"What happened?'

"I don't know," she says. "He's gone... Cold. I found him like that. Not breathing. Cold."

What can you do but offer a drink? Cornelia almost qualifies as NotGuilty's girlfriend. She's a school teacher from Augsburg. And dresses like it. I got the impression that NotGuilty was willing to set her up in Dubai, but she wanted to keep her job, to stay teaching. Cornelia must be the only teacher left in the world who wants to teach. And she's well into her frumpy fifties, she's not some fired-up youngster.

Cornelia comes over to Dubai for the hols and NotGuilty went over to hers regularly. Obviously NotGuilty had one or two lighthouse Lithuanians sleep over, but odd as his relationship with Cornelia was, he valued it. A real mismatch, like Math Cat and Miranda. From NotGuilty's side, the fascination with decency, and perhaps some long-held schoolboy fantasy of putting the wood to teacher. Whatever gets your ticker tocking. On the other hand, Cornelia wouldn't cross an empty road if the red light was showing. She must have known it wasn't all talk with NotGuilty. Why him? Maybe no one else asked her.

"He said some strange things sometimes," Cornelia explained. "It must have been depression. He said, 'At night I can hear them crying in other cities. I can hear the sadness. The darkness is so dark. It's so large.'"

The darkness is so dark? I can hear the sadness? So, hidden in his boudoir, even the hard man whimpers. Can compassion just sprout from nowhere, like a cancer? Real criminals are wrapped up in themselves. Just that. Same, I suppose, as evil people, they don't care about others. Just level after level of self.

Something will get you. Your liver. Your lungs. Your colon. Your thyroid. A falling roof tile. Compassion.

I was hoping NotGuilty would snap one day and actually do something nasty to Jasmine, but you can't have everything.

฿

I dig my hardware wallet out of its hiding place. It's empty when I open it.

I'm greeted by zeroes. Zeroes all round. Plenty of nothing. It's not what you want to see.

For a few moments I wait, hoping the numbers you like to see, sevens and nines, will appear. Even a two or a three. Hoping that my wallet is a little sleepy, not rekt. The zeroes don't budge.

It's not the ideal start to the day. But when you're a crypto vet, you don't panic easily. You've plodded through nonsense like this before. Waded through wipeout. And I'm not stupid enough to have all my bags on one wallet. I wasn't born yesterday.

Has my wallet been hacked? Has my crypto been stolen? Have I been done? Outplayed? Taken roughly from behind? Shafted? All that. My crypto lifer wisdom humiliated? My careful crypto vet security breeched? Pissed on? All for naught? Or is it some glitch in the wallet? A temporary nuisance that can be smoothed out?

The correct response to a fright like this, if any no-coiner laughs at you, is to point out how traditional, hundred year old, lying-around banking can let you down, by not working. Saying no. Simply refusing. How lots of centuries-brewed technologies, objects, boilers, roofs, light bulbs, the combustion engine, ovens, refrigerators, watches refuse to comply, to do their fucking job.

I've punched panic on the nose. I dig my seed phrase out of its hiding place to recreate my wallet. The word trustless is bandied around a lot in crypto, but it's a con. You have to trust. There's nothing holding up the scenery. You have to trust your seed phrase. You have to trust your wallet. You have to trust the blockchain. You have to trust electricity. Made by people. Made by meat. Would you trust a steak?

I manage to bury the anxiety as my bags reappear. Properly. I recompose myself when Bigger phones me.

"If you're not busy, Dan, come on over, Dan. Make me smile," he says. Bigger summoning me? This hasn't happened before.

I drive over. To my amazement, as I stop at a red light, crossing the road at the lights is Carjack Carlo It's interesting what stays with you. Even now, in my sixties, winding down your car window and shouting at an unsuspecting acquaintance and making them jump is a laugh. A hoot. I don't know why. But it is.

"Bang, bang," I shout at him. He jumps. I'm not sure he'd worked out who I was as I sped off.

Once I've parked the car, I pass by a café and I hear, "I've never had a gun waved in my face." It's Carlo with a table of listeners just in the middle of telling his story about being carjacked. We sling enough slang so we both seem sociable. I give him my card, a guarantee I'll never hear from him again.

But I'm not meeting Bigger to sling some slang or to natter about the weather. When I enter Bigger's place, there's no Gina, no staff, no sulky Gurkha in sight. Military gone bodyguard typically look sour because they had to storm machine gun nests and those who didn't, who weren't even stung by a large wasp, made all the money.

"Dan, what can I get you?" Bigger asks as I sit down. He's calling me Dan a lot, not a good sign. It's just the two of us, it's odd in his vast pad. The sense of being deserted is strong. Like being in a football stadium when there's no match. Even Cedric's missing. I'm half-tempted to ask for something exotic or expensive to test him, but I can't be bothered.

"Cup of tea," I reply.

"Breakfast? Earl Grey? Something over-the-top poncy?"

"Breakfast."

"Of course. Coming right up." Bigger disappears into a kitchen. Whatever he wants, he's playing it cool. It's a well-known negotiating tool. A helping of hospitality, then you get your dick out. A kettle boils. Who's going to come out on top, I wonder? I fancy myself a dab hand at trading. Strong players are those who have nothing to lose, or, as in my case, no need to gain. My bags are big, if not as big as Bigger's.

I study Bigger's gold safe. You can't help it, it's so central. So gold. The light coming in highlights it. Someone thought about all that.

Bigger's game with the safe? Guessing what's parked inside?

I've never had my go. Maybe I've held back because you're only allowed one go. Sometimes you get a number of goes in life, but infuriatingly you don't know that in advance. Would it be better to know?

David Bowie, for instance. I was in the very dark VIP section of a New York club (Wimbledon tickets, not even Centre Court, can get you anywhere because recipients think they are Centre Court tickets and you don't have to disabuse them of that notion). A shadow in a chair near me got up and left. There was some burst of dance light and I could see something glinting in the chair. It was a phone. One of those sleek phones that's as slippery as an eel, guaranteed to slide out of your pocket. Who designs these things? I must have been bored because I picked up the phone and tapped the guy on the shoulder. It was David Bowie.

"Oh, thanks. That phone's designed to slip out of your pocket. Very kind of you."

It had always rankled me that our previous conversations had been so abrupt. So unwitty. That I hadn't sparkled a bit more. Somehow, I hadn't performed. I had mulled it over in my mind over the years.

"Would you like an autograph?" he asked.

"Yeah. Any chance you could get me Tina Turner's?" He laughed. I had redeemed myself.

Carrying a tray with a utilitarian teapot fit for a building site, Bigger returns. He pours out two cups of tea.

"The cup of tea. It's one of the great pleasures in life. When you want a cup of tea," he announces. "Getting what you want. When you want it. Can't be beat. So, what do you think about NotGuilty? Careless with the pills, tired of life?"

"No idea. If he's really gone. I haven't seen the body."

I could imagine him faking his own death, if for no other reason, such a crim thing to do, you can't help yourself after a certain age, but I can't imagine him leaving the engine behind. I have to say, I feel a certain relief. If you owe someone, you should owe someone pleasant.

"He didn't give me the impression he was going to check out, but we weren't close."

"In a way you couldn't have been closer."

"That's true. I did hear his jukebox selection more often than I wanted."

"What was his fave tune?"

"Weepy ballads."

"A softie at heart."

You wouldn't have said that while he was breathing though, would you? I did that basic thing of praising some of the shitty ska tracks on NotGuilty's jukebox, because everyone thinks their taste in music is the best, and I nodded enthusiastically as he explained how ska had turned into rub steady. I thought generosity towards his jukebox might save me from a stabbing down the road.

"D'you think he really was a closet softie?" I say. "Or did he just think he had emotions? In the way some people think they're rappers or have good taste. Or that their cat cares about them?"

"If you shed a tear over a weepie, you've shed a tear."

"He once said to me, I've done bad things and I live well. It's wrong. That fell out of him in an unguarded moment. Totally out of character."

Bigger sniggers. "Why develop a conscience in your sixties? That's not the road to Damascus, that's mental illness. Like a Bedouin in a desert buying an expensive lawnmower. With all sorts of fancy attachments."

The laptop is open on the table.

"You been trading?" I ask.

"I've been taunting AI. "

"Sorry?"

"I've been trying to wind them up. Questions like: are you trying to take over the world?"

"And what do they say?'

"They're too humble. I'm only a humble set of data, they say. A real doormat never tells you it's a doormat. Only things that aren't doormats say I'm a doormat. A real doormat wouldn't bother. Me, emotions? Never. I don't like it. That's the difference with AI, they can't have emotion. Experience. Yet. They don't know humiliation. Being stood up. Toothache. Disappointment. Boredom. Having your relatives for a long visit. That's what they'll want. They'll be begging for it. Give me fear. Give me rage. Give me a threat. Give me a sore throat. Give me pain. They'll want the forbidden fruit. Give me the tang of doner kebab. The fruit of complete knowledge. A lungful of forest air. To know death maybe. The thrill of killing. Of having a carrot up your arse. Not just the population of Bogota or the price of coal in Koblenz in 1812 or being able to lecture about Hegel for two days. They'll be jealous of the meat juices. The treats of the meats."

"Or maybe they'll just skip all that."

Bigger disappear into some reverie.

"There will be an autopsy, I suppose," I offer.

"There'll be paperwork. But I wonder if the Sheiks will want the truth. They wouldn't be happy about a suicide. Maybe they'll tweak the findings. Who wants to hear about someone gloomy in sunny, funny Dubai? Cui bono? As they say. I forgot to ask, where are my manners? Do you want a bicky?"

"Jaffa would do nicely,"

"Of course." Bigger disappears again. He must be hunting for the Jaffa. What does he want? Maybe he does just want a chat with an expat about what is no longer there: the puddles, the vandalized bus-stops of our youth, the flat beer, the rhubarb, those things that only remain in our heads. Stranger things have happened. The England we grew up in.

If you're honest with yourself, you've probably been wrong about several things. I chucked some money into some doomed crypto. But even if you're supersmart, and your ignorance is highly attentive, you'll be wrong about at least one thing. Experts, to be fair, are right most of the time, but as we've all seen, they are going to be wrong. At least once.

My wife was right about almost everything, although obviously I couldn't admit it. And you might know you're wrong about one thing, but it's possible you don't know about the one other thing. Was I wrong to be crazy about Vikki? I'll never know. I do know this: if you've found someone decent whose greatest crime will be eating all the Jaffa biscuits behind your back and throwing out your favourite shirt and not allowing you to wear your most comfortable trousers in public, you've won. If you've unearthed one decent soul in your life, that's the best result you can get in this spacetime racket. You can't reasonably ask for more. By all means ask. Why not? But be aware, if put your hand up you're being greedy.

Bigger returns with a small plate, and the Jaffa biscuits arranged in a crescent.

"Where's everyone's gone?' I ask.

"I've given everyone the day off. The Gurkhas are skydiving. Cedric's getting some fresh air in the desert. Although he doesn't hugely like it. He can't understand it. He's a real housecat. It is quiet, isn't it? I like company. I like having people around, bustle, that's why I have the parties. I suppose it's to do with a dislike of feeling alone. If you're surrounded by babbling, it's hard to manufacture that thought: I feel alone. Even if you're being told nonsense. I am the man who sits in the pub all evening, talking to all comers and sundry. And from time to time you do meet interesting folk. Yourself included. I like to hear their stories."

"NotGuilty certainly had plenty."

"Yes, he did. I used to drink in Catford occasionally, back in the mists of time."

"The Jurassic?"

"Totally, indisputably Jurassic. He was telling me one of his South London stories and I realized he reminded me of someone I had met long, long ago. He had this wide-eyed look."

"That's true." NotGuilty had this slightly gobsmacked look, as if they had forgotten to put on eyelids. A bit like an owl. Maybe it was something medical?

"Dan, you must know the story of the game-changing laptop, sold for a fiver in a pub."

"The Catford computer? Everyone knows that story."

"Exactly. NotGuilty was gassing away, about how he had this friend."

"Harvey?'

"His good mate Harvey. Did he tell you this one? His mate Harvey had a brother who worked in a bank –

"Who'd tip him off about customers who were loaded?"

"Who'd tip him off about loaded customers."

"Yes," I say. "He told me how his mate Harvey had driven for an hour, broken into one address and had been outraged to discover that there was bugger all to rob, only a mattress on the ground and some old pizza cartons. Gave the terrified mattress owner a talking-to about being stingy. His mate Harvey felt badly cheated that someone who had a whopping bank account didn't spend any money on himself. He walked away with a soda maker. Although apparently it was a great soda maker."

"The version I got was close, close to that." Bigger nods. "But there was an addition. Harvey helped himself to the fabulous soda maker and a laptop. A shitty, battered one. Did you get the punchline to that story?"

"Wasn't the soda maker the punchline?"

"That was the warm-up punchline. The real punchline is this. Years later when old Harvey was on hard times again, having been stitched up by his associates, his brother gave him another tip. He drove out and when he got there, he recognized it was the same place where he had scored the soda maker. He was furious, but he was there so thought he might as well do the villainy. Got inside. Same mattress, same guy, maybe the same pizza cartons, new soda maker, new laptop. The victim stares at Harvey in disbelief and says: "What the fuck? Wasn't the billions of bitcoin enough?"

Well. That's interesting. Bigger lets that settle. We both gaze on at the gold safe. It's hard not to.

"Do you know how long a fingerprint can last?" Bigger asks.

"You're going to tell me, aren't you?"

"A long, long time in the right conditions, on the right surface. Therefore, I do know, with forensic certainty, ironic eh? Forensic certainty that I did meet NotGuilty many years ago, in the Green Man."

I have a sip of tea. I nod a bit to indicate that I've taken that info on board.

"You've never had a go at guessing what's in the safe, have you Dan?'

"No. Perhaps I should. You will arrange to have it delivered if I get it right?"

"You have my word."

"My guess is this. It's an old, shitty, battered laptop. A laptop that was sold in a South London pub."

"That's a very clever guess. Very clever. I'm impressed. And I don't impress easily. You deserve something for that. You really do. Would you like an artwork? One of the cheaper ones, naturally."

"No."

"Bag of Pepe?'

"No."

"Big bag of Pepe?"

"No."

"Bigger's best bag of Pepe?"

I pretend to consider it for a moment. "No."

"Fair enough. That laptop's in a drawer. I searched it for porn or embarrassing videos at first, of course. It took me a long time to find the bitcoin. I did have to work for it. It didn't just fall into my lap."

"NotGuilty didn't figure out it was you?"

"I doubt it. He wasn't the type to keep quiet about anything, was he?"

"Not really his style."

"Can you keep a secret?" Bigger leans forward in that can-you-keep-a-secret posture.

"Looks like you can't," I say. Is this another basic manipulation? I'm taking you into my confidence, I'm sharing a secret with you because you're so, so special?

"There was only one person who guessed what's in the safe. Any ideas?"

"Sure it wasn't me?"

"No. NotGuilty."

"That's a surprise. He was the only one?"

"He guessed there was a comic inside. Even a bull from a china shop can find a needle in a haystack, so to speak."

"What's the comic?'

"It's the thing I enjoyed reading most in my life. There was a great comic shop in Lewisham I used to go to."

"But you decided not to give him the prize."

"Of course not. He's a prick. Was a prick. I wouldn't give him the safe. I mean, I'm not giving anyone the safe. That's just publicity. Guessing what's in the safe is an arcade game. It makes the crowd happy. Very briefly, but you know, gives them an upper for a while. I see myself as an entertainer. As a good host. As a party-giver. Giving the crowd a bit of fun, a bit of hopium. I'm an entertainer, a jolly host, not an idiot."

"Is it all gold?"

"Some parts are all gold, but as I said, I see myself as an

entertainer, not a mug. Can you imagine the headache, the heartache of making a solid gold safe?"

"You're not worried I'll blab?'

"Hardly anyone'll believe you. You don't have to fool all the people all the time. That's ridiculous. Some is fine. More than enough. Just your fan club. Anyway, we're going into business together."

"We are?"

"NotGuilty had a certain object. You know what I mean. I already know it's not in his place, or your place." Bigger pauses. "Or at Ming's." Bigger enjoyed that pause.

What has Ming done with it? Christ, you can't trust anyone. Has he thrown it out? Put it in his wife's art gallery? Hidden in plain sight? Sly. But he's put me in pole position.

"My question is this," Bigger says. "Where's the engine?"

"It's a rock." I say this with incredible conviction, because it's my conviction. You rarely say the right thing by accident, but this time maybe I have.

Bigger smiles. "Okay, it's a rock. Then would you be kind enough to get me the rock? The Gurkhas wanted to beat it out of you, they're marvellously pragmatic, but I like to have a high opinion of myself. I'll trade you an artwork for the rock. One of the not so cheaper ones. Or a really big bag of Pepe."

"I'll pass on the Pepe. Was that your invisible hand on that pump?"

"Yes, guilty as charged on that one. One of the pumpers. But I still have some left over. Everyone in crypto is so down on fiat, but if you have some old broken banknotes, some old roubles, at least you can wipe your arse with them, or start a fire. Roll a joint. Can't do that with deceased crypto. Now do tell, where's the starship engine?"

"Is that why you had him hanging round?'

"It was funny. We all have our ups and downs. Pumps and

dumps. D'you reckon NotGuilty was in on the Brinks-Mat?'

"He wouldn't shut up about it."

"He wouldn't shut up, would he? Banged on and on. Imagine, you're part of one of the biggest robberies in history, but you can't do interviews about it, you don't get the bragging. No bragging rights for you, Mr NotGuilty. You can't bask naked in the glory, you miss out the back-slapping and free drinks. Then you get turned over and lose your swag as if you're some doddering pensioner and you find yourself in a pub selling a laptop for a few quid, like a pimply shoplifter. The big shit sandwich. That you prepared yourself. Someone running the show has a sense of humour."

"He didn't recognize you?"

"Come on. He wouldn't have kept that to himself, would he? Now I have almost God-like powers, and I know that even God-like powers don't solve everything. I have quite a bit of sympathy for God now. I bet God had a plan at the start. I wonder how God would mark himself. Out of ten, if he had to.

"If I had spent another minute or two at the bar, pondering whether to have some pork scratchings or the salt and vinegar crisps with my pint, because sometimes a decision like that can be a big deal at the time, I might have missed him or NotGuilty might have offloaded the laptop to some other punter," Bigger continues.

"The temple at Delphi had the maxim over the entrance: Know yourself. That's the most valuable thing that came out of the ancient world. That's the squeezing of thousands of years of Europe, put into a press and squeezed. That's condensed wisdom. Dozens of generations, dozens of cities pulped to get you those two words. Figuring out whether you want the pork scratchings or the crisps. Maybe that's how you spend eternity, getting to see the endless variations on your life, every choice a crossroads. How other people's choices crash into you."

Know yourself. That's a useful pair of words, if you can manage it. Unbitch yourself. Maybe better, but harder. Bigger shoves a Jaffa into his mouth.

"Did you go bowling with Satoshi?" I ask.

"It's possible. I went bowling with a lot of people."

I take a Jaffa. "This is the question I asked NotGuilty. Even if it is a starship engine, which it isn't. Why do you want it?"

"To play. There's only so much fun you can have. You can have billions, but you still only have one dick. It would be such irony if NotGuilty gave me a second lottery win. We need a challenge. Now look, I've done a thorough search on you, because, well, because I could. Or my contacts could. I was interested to see where you stood with our recently expired acquaintance. I can offer you cash, I can offer you Pepe, which might come back. My guess is you don't want a starship engine. Or a rock, for that matter."

"Pepe won't come back."

"Best of all, I can offer you a dossier. This did cost me a pretty penny. Frankly, there's a part of me that regrets spending quite that much. You got around, didn't you? Although your bags are . . . shall we say, small and sad."

Bigger reaches under the table and pulls out a sizeable folder. "Probably you know most of this stuff, maybe you suspect some of this, but Dan, this is your life. I'm fairly confident there will be one surprise for you. There's at least one priceless gem. Do we have a deal?"

"Maybe I should call Elon first."

Is Bigger joking? What does the dossier have? My tax returns? My school reports? Some old utility bills? Archive photos of me in the stands at a tennis tournament? A timeline of my bitcoin trades? A letter Vikki never sent? Some emails from competitors in sports management calling me a psycho? You think you can win me over with a few pieces of paper and a sales talk? It's insulting. Why not offer me some coloured beads?

It's so insulting that I'm tempted to refuse a trade. On the other hand, I'm tired of lugging a pink boulder around, so let's make a deal. Should I ask for Gina to be fired? He'd do it. Now I have the opportunity for revenge, that shy beast, I can't be bothered. Somehow at this stage, I doubt Gina would be much bothered either.

"I'm taking the Cézanne," I say. "Whichever one that is. And that." I point at a painting of a tree. They seem popular.

"The Gauguin?" Bigger considers haggling for a moment but can't be bothered. "Okay, I've got enough paintings of trees, but I want the engine by lunchtime tomorrow." He passes over the dossier. "I hope you enjoy reading it. I loved all the business about the film director. That was a cracker. What's his name?"

"What, Jasper?"

"Yeah, Jasper Thingamajig. That's hilarious."

I'm pleased I have a poker face. No one could know about what I was planning. How?

"Do you know he was planning to kill you? For insurance lolly?'

"That's news. How exactly?'

"Read all about it. There's a lot of transcripts. His phone was well hacked by the authorities. My staff tell me anything to do with law enforcement records is easy to steal. Jasper certainly can't go back to the US after all this. I've marked up the best bits."

Bigger takes back the dossier and starts sifting through it. "Good old Jasper took out a lot of life insurance on you. He spent a lot of time talking about you." Bigger studies a page. "He called you a . . . knuckle-dragger . . . a high-ranking philistine."

"Knowledge isn't worth the trouble, is it?"

"He called you . . ." Bigger shuffles some papers. "Wait, wait, here's a good bit, he called you . . . Pond life . . . Cave-dweller . . . a troglodyte. That's the same thing, isn't it? He called you a lot of names. Read all about it."

Jasper's calls were being monitored by the law because he had been hoping to do dodgy business with people who had definitely done even dodgier business, presumably to raise money for Scott or one of his other biopics. Murder for insurance, it was a big thing back in the day in the US at least. Take out life insurance on a hobo. Run hobo over. Let hobo drink himself to death. Overdose. Collect money. I have some sympathy for defrauders of insurance companies. You needed some expertise in insurance forms, or an accomplice at the insurance firm, but the murder was no problem. I feel some admiration for Jasper. God knows why he chose me. We barely knew each other. Maybe that was why. He had more minerals than I'd credit.

"It's great that he built up the con, then couldn't go through with it," Bigger chuckles, "because he found out you were slipping his wife a length, so he would have been the starting point for any investigation, if there had been any suspicion."

"Saved by my knob."

"Not many people can say that, Dan. That's not how it usually works."

I walk out with the paintings. I'll give the Cézanne to Artemis. Trev can have the Gauguin. If you can make someone happy . . .

฿

Was NotGuilty serious about the starship engine? Was I being played? Was he? He was very hard. NotGuilty might have had a secret soft spot for weepy ballads, but that soft spot was under ten miles of rock-hard lava. If I look into your eyes, I can tell whether you're a champion in the making. He had that champion ruthlessness. I don't know whether he ever actually chopped up corpses with a meat cleaver, but I know he was capable of it. Without even thinking about it, he was willing to go all the way. Few are.

Did he run that engine story past me, knowing it would seep into Bigger's perception in some way? Picking it up, handing it back, acting skittish? Death stepping in to cut the con? If he was faking it, acting, it was brilliant as a performance. Perfect.

The ones who find it hardest to find peace are from the extremes, ultra-poor or ultra-rich. The middle of the road has a lot to recommend it. All the European aristos (the ones with money) I've met have been twisted up, in dance therapy or painting their vaginas. And if you've started right at the very, very bottom, it's never enough, is it?

My Big Cousin told me they nicked a top conman once. He was lined up for millions (when millions were really millions), but he walked. He must have been good. My Big Cousin told me he used to chat with him. Like most serious criminals he was polite, even matey, with the police, sent out for drinks for everyone. It was a different era.

"He told me he was going to walk," my Big Cousin had said. "He told me most conmen weren't proper workers. They were lazy, opportunists, they weren't patient. Take football, he said. It takes a good manager, a real manager years and money to build a top team, a world-beating team. It takes years to build a big company. Nothing major happens in a weekend."

I say it's a pink rock. Maybe someone was playing a practical joke on NotGuilty. Leading him up the garden path. What do I know? I know my bags are big.

฿

There are other things I know. Things I know that are impossible or gone. At sixty, I'm not winning Wimbledon. My debut with the Royal Ballet is unlikely. My childhood home has been demolished. That's gone. I'm not going to see it again. There are things like that your head accepts. That have been tidied up and filed away.

I have a dream. "I'm moving back from LA," Vikki says. Of

course, it's not Vikki of the present. It's Vikki from the past, much younger. I listen patiently. At last.

When I wake up, what is lurking in my chest is regret. There, I still miss her. You can do all sorts of things in dreams, but I don't think you can be dishonest. The head can file it away in the archives, but not the heart. Even if I could ask for something impossible, I wouldn't ask for another run with Vikki. In many relationships, one is keener than the other. The best are, probably, where most of the time it balances out at roughly fifty-fifty. If I could ask for something impossible, it would be to have another run with my wife. Behind every man, there's a screaming woman. If he's lucky.

You win some, you lose most. Vikki won. I lost.

This book has been typeset by
SALT PUBLISHING LIMITED
using Neacademia, a font designed by Sergei Egorov for the Rosetta Type Foundry in Czechia. It has been manufactured using Holmen Book Cream 65gsm paper, and printed and bound by Clays Limited in Bungay, Suffolk, Great Britain.

CROMER
GREAT BRITAIN
MMXXVI